THE SUN RISES IN EASTMOOR

CALVIN NILES

The Sun Rises in Eastmoor

By Calvin Niles

www.calvinniles.com

Paperback ISBN: 978-1-9196509-0-6

Copyright © Calvin Niles 2020

Published by The Mindful Storyteller, 2021

For Nicola Springer

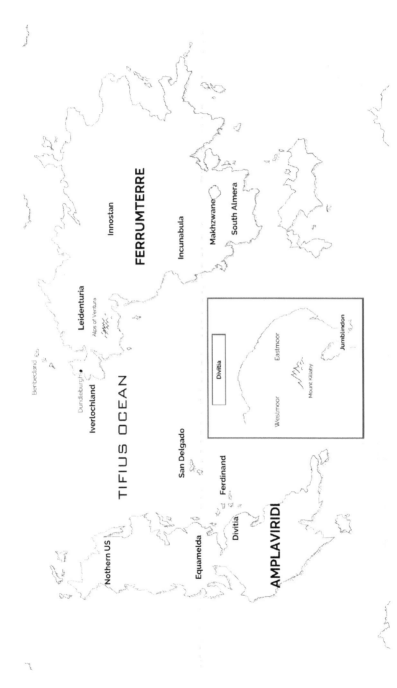

Table of Contents

CHAPTER 1 1

CHAPTER 2 13

CHAPTER 3 17

CHAPTER 4 23

CHAPTER 5 35

CHAPTER 6 45

CHAPTER 7 61

CHAPTER 8 67

CHAPTER 9 73

CHAPTER 10 87

CHAPTER 11 103

CHAPTER 12 115

CHAPTER 13 119

CHAPTER 14 133

CHAPTER 15 137

CHAPTER 16 153

CHAPTER 17 159

CHAPTER 18 169

CHAPTER 19 177

CHAPTER 20 187

CHAPTER 21 193

CHAPTER 22 215

CHAPTER 23 223

CHAPTER 24 231

CHAPTER 25 235

ACKNOWLEDGEMENTS 241

ABOUT THE AUTHOR... 243

CHAPTER 1

The flight back to Divitia was mostly pleasant, bar our penetration through the cloud base on the approach to Moorland International. Towering clouds turned the interior of the aircraft from brilliant to bleak in a matter of just a few meters. I knew well to put my handkerchief over my nose during this phase of the flight since the aroma of cheese, coffee and vomit only created—well—more vomit. It was not quite hurricane season in the region yet, but tropical clouds make for violent descents at any time of the year. There were black rubber bulges on the wing surfaces that expanded and contracted, breaking the ice forming from its edges. Those passengers whose views were not obscured by sick bags watched the valiant attempts of each super-cooled water droplet to envelop us in an icy tomb. Meanwhile, I stared at my fingernails, remembering the events that took place just before I departed.

I was in my room at the Royal Botanical Hotel. A

racket outside, someone banging on a door, startled me out of my mid-morning nap. My heart galloped as my eyelids flew open, their insides sanding my eyeballs to a gritty finish. Clinging to opportunities for sleep did that to the eyes.

"Room thirty-three is it?" asked a deep voice softly.

"It appears he's not in, sir," a female voice responded.

"Would you like me to call reception to get a key?" asked another.

My dilated pupils offered no protection from the equatorial sunlight blasting through the window. Those blackout drapes were useless thanks to their jammed runners. Nothing offered by the hotel was compensatory-enough, not even the room upgrade I was given. King-sized deluxe suites were normal for me by then.

While the brilliant white ceiling blinded me, nothing could deafen me to the commotion in the hallway.

"Two-four-one, what is your status, over?"

"Get reception up here with that key!"

I guessed it was the police in the hallway, looking for the guy in the room next to mine. My fright and disorientation tailed off somewhat, even as their sense of urgency was growing.

"This is the only way, it's the only way! I have to do this," said an agitated voice coming through the wall. A strong determination modulated his tone.

The shouting in the corridor made the walls seem paper thin, despite the celebrated five-star hotel charging a premium for 'total silence or your money back'.

"All will be revealed soon enough! The truth behind the Citizen Science program will eventually come out, and you will all see for yourself!" the police target screamed.

Pictures ran through my mind like wild stallions, conjuring all the possibilities of what he might be trying to say, and why the police were after him. An instinctive empathy manifested in my body as goosebumps. *There are some crazy people out there,* I thought.

After three months in The Royal Botanical, the finest hotel in Equamelda, it was not unusual to connect with another regular guest, even those to whom you had never spoken. You could even say it was comforting for those of us who worked away from home a lot. But this guy was different. Plus, his strange behaviour and saccadic movements kept most people at bay.

"They told me to go beneath the surface. They told me to find the truth. You dickheads have no idea what is really going on, do you? With your safe jobs, cushy pensions, and on-demand lifestyle. I'm willing to go all the way to expose the truth!" the agitated voice came again.

Avoiding the squeaking floorboards near the door required precision, and at the entrance, I peered out through the peephole into the corridor. I was energised by more than a passing interest—it was rather a bubbling inquisitiveness that pulled me to see what was going on. It was not the first time I had come across strange ones.

There was just enough light for me to make out eight of them. The two in front were in riot gear, bearing shields and scowling faces. Standing well over six feet tall, they squatted behind their defences with their uniforms bulging in places that suggested superhuman strength. A young man joined the group panting and handed a key over to the Sergeant.

"It's not working!" yelled the lead officer in frustration at the barricaded door. "We're going to have to break it down, step back."

"Citizen Science is a smoke screen, you'll see!"

"Sir, we are just policemen doing our job. We don't know what you are talking about, nor do we care, just open up or we'll have to break it down. And you'll be paying in the end."

As events intensified, my muscles squeezed my

skeleton like a constrictor around its prey. I winced, stepping back from the door to avoid seeing what my imagination already had. My memory was stained enough already.

One step back, then two, then bang! An explosion rocked the room.

"Go-go-go!" The stampeding officers entered room thirty-three.

Screeching, groaning, the abrasive sounds of police uniforms rubbing against the walls in a tussle. A rumbling of bodies, pants of exertion and yelling. Half of the screams were police instructions to comply, the other half protestations of denial from a man losing his mind.

Two four one to control, we got him, over…"

Back at the peephole, a picture of a man being handled down the hallway in handcuffs squeezed through. He looked towards my door, exhausted and maniacal, with a deep sadness underlying his glances.

Surely, he can't see me, can he?

"The Elders told me to look into it, they told me to find out what lies beneath the surface. They did. Yes, they did."

Conspiracy gobbledegook was a favourite past-time of mine. Starting from the secret sects and architects of financial Ponzi schemes to the power families of Leidenturia to name but a few powerful groups bent on world domination—I was fascinated by them all. But I had never heard about the Elders.

It was a scarring end to the big government project I was glad to be done with and the few winks I stole before my return flight were welcome.

Life was great and despite missing my sons, Dante and Eli, each day gave at least one moment of joy. I was no stranger to the odd drama on work trips—I remember another oddball here from the past—but this episode stood out especially, and I couldn't wait to get home to tell Sasha all about it. Working for a pool of demanding, sometimes narcissistic, clients between frequent business flights and time away from my family had a way of depleting my energy. Yet I always had just enough left in reserve to pine for them. Five-star accommodation, silver service and day-round happy hours could not dull my longing and, with another consulting project done, it was homeward bound to the wife and kids.

"Cabin crew, ten minutes to landing," announced the captain.

The wings flexed and danced under the disco effect of lights refracting around the inside of the cloud. Naturally, only the flight-crew, flight attendants and seasoned travellers acclimatised to this chaotic routine.

How ironic that most people below were sweating in tropical heat while our aircraft battled with the polar Gods. It always fascinated me that such extreme opposites could exist in the same place at the same time.

My handkerchief filtered the stench floating around the aircraft cabin, at the same time amplifying my visions of home, of Sasha. It kept her sweet scent well after all that time away. She had this thing of spraying her perfume onto select items in secret and slipping them into my travel bag for me to discover at random times. I could already feel her cheeks in my palms and the weight of two excited lumps on my back doing what they could to drag me into the floor. Dante and Eli were the little gems that kept me going.

What interesting escapades have you got to share then, babe? I imagined Sash's first question. Stories and pillow talk were one of my post-work highlights and we had a lot to catch up on. But I was not home yet and my memories were still ablaze.

"Fasten your seatbelt please, sir," demanded the steward.

"Sure," I complied and returned swiftly to the thought of how I might describe the crazy guy to Sasha, how he escaped the clutches of all those police officers and charged almost a full 12 stories up to the roof of the hotel. It was extraordinary. The shrieking scream of a young, injured officer pushed me back from the peephole to the temporary relief of my window at the other end of the room, where I stood squinting outwards.

The sun left nothing unscathed in Equamelda. Stone ornaments were bleached to an astonishing white, and the wooden handrails around the seating area rejected the paint unanimously. A fading sound of marching boots filing out of the corridor ushered in a moment of welcomed quiet.

Beneath my window, the Albizia tree released a flock of blackbirds in a flourish. Then a large flash of darkness flew by my window, pulling my eyes down behind it. I looked past the blistering paint on the outside of my window ledge and I spotted him. Well, he was unrecognisable, contorted into painful-looking shapes, with his head the wrong way round. But his clothes were unmistakable. They served a new purpose now—part bag, part sponge—holding his parts in one place, while soaking up his blood and other fluids. There was no ceremony, no final showdown, nothing. The officers were still probably catching their breath somewhere between my floor and the roof. Pity. Trying to wash that image from my mind would be like trying to unbreathe my last breath. But just as my mind became stained, it became inquiring. *What torment would bring this soul to take his own life?*

My mind stopped for a moment, pulled back into the aircraft by the electric sound of the motor lowering the wheels of the landing gear. Below, our land—like the heads of broccoli—looked like virgin territory. Large green space, dense with vegetation and mountains spread across the continent. Amplaviridi was the home to Divitia, and Eastmoor, where I was born and raised.

"Ladies and gentlemen, welcome to Moorland International," announced the captain.

A sudden applause broke out at the rear of the cabin. The wheels of the aircraft kissed the tarmac so gently I barely noticed. After speedy disembarkation, the Divitian Ports Authority checked our passports and welcomed us all back to Divitia. Only the customs hall stood between me and my chauffeur.

"Welcome home Mr. Vincent," Tim greeted me in the arrivals hall. "How was your flight?" He grabbed hold of my suit carrier and I followed him.

"Thanks, Tim, it feels good to be home."

"Nothing like home, is there?"

"It's called sweet home for a reason, right?" I replied.

The drive back from the airport was painless though it certainly did not need such a beast of Leidenturian engineering for such a short ride. I bet those taxi contracts cost the company a fortune. Even the large toads hopping from puddle to puddle as they crossed the pot-holed streets would have considered getting squashed by the 20-inch tires an honour. I counselled myself that there was nothing wrong with a little more luxurious time in which I could sit and process the weird altercation that happened back at the Botanical.

From any perspective, the man in the hotel was nuts. With time, my thoughts of him transformed from concern to intrigue and—strangely—into a kind of excitement. Sasha often revelled in my stories, and I loved to tell them. He was disturbed, yes, but it was what he was obsessed about that stuck in my throat like a fine fishbone. I kept seeing his face through that peephole with his screaming assertions about "the truth" ringing in my ears. Whatever that meant.

Anyway, more pressing matters loomed and in minutes we pulled up outside my house. Tim failed in his efforts to get to my car door before I could open it myself. Thankfully, the streets in my neighbourhood had better drainage than the dilapidated roads we had to pass to get there. I hated grey skies almost as much as getting my shoes dirty.

"Stay there, Tim." I insisted. "No point us both getting wet. Let me save you a trip to the dry cleaners."

"Thank you, sir. Hope to see you again in a few weeks' time."

The car pulled away silently behind me. As I walked up to the front door of our home, insects competed for the best song, accompanied by the hi-hats of water displacing beneath my leather soles. Besides that, it was eerily quiet. *Perhaps they are inside playing one of their pranks.*

"I'm home!" I yelled, barging past the heavy oak door.

But the house was still.

"Hello! Erm, hello?" Where is everyone? Gotcha!" I jumped around the corner in anticipation of Eli hiding behind the wall. There were a few apparitions, but no one for me to touch and hold, to thrust into the air, to cuddle or to kiss.

Something was definitely wrong. Scanning my immediate vicinity, I found a folded piece of paper lay on the marble kitchen counter. Sculpted like the perfect piece of origami, it awaited me:

"Dear Leo,

I'm sorry it had to be done this way but any other way would have been a lot worse for the kids. There is someone else, someone who can be there for me when I need them—someone who makes me feel alive. I know you will survive; you always had that in you. At some point when things settle down for us both, I'll contact you about the kids. I will always have a special place in my heart for you Leo, but what we had was never enough.

Take care of yourself. I'm sorry.

Sasha."

CHAPTER 2

Since I read Sasha's letter, time passed like treacle through a sieve. *Welcome to your new reality, Leo,* became my new mantra. Meaningful life-progress could be measured in nanoseconds or even Plancks. The space between my bedroom and the kitchen stayed warmer than the rest of the house due to the friction from my constant marching to and fro'. The house telephone would ring from time to time, but I refused to answer it because I knew it would not be her. Sasha had not taken any of my calls in the three months since I discovered her note. My calls to her numbered in the thousands by then. Soon after I gave up trying, I stopped jumping every time the phone rang. Sometimes I would hear from my mother though, whose concern for me knew no bounds. She did not need to contact me by phone, because we had a telepathic connection. She always spoke to me telepathically. It was weird to some but to me, without it, would be like imagining my life without gravity.

"Leo, have you considered my suggestion?"

"Hi Mum. Ye...yes, I have. I've started to engage with the university but it's still early days," I said. *What else will I do?* I thought, and fixed myself a fresh cup of coffee. Nothing else worked to rid me of morning headaches like Divitian black, steaming with hints of chocolate and blueberry.

"Good," she replied. "I am sure that the Citizen Science program will give you some much needed purpose right now."

"You don't need to worry about me, Mum. I'm doing fine." I said my usual reply to anyone who enquired about me.

On the small kitchen bookshelf where I kept the coffee, a framed Father's Day card from Dante stopped me. It was one of his hand-drawn creations. This one depicted the day we did the fund-raising walk-up Mount Killaby—the whole family together, smiling and so happy.

Purpose. I thought, gripping the mug between my gnawed fingertips. My mother's words lingered.

* * *

The crowd science research program was unfolding

all over the continent, though my own involvement had just begun. I remembered hearing that term before my mother mentioned it, Citizen Science, back at the Royal Botanical before it receded into a distant part of my mind. But when it returned, it became much more significant, especially after I met Frasier that same night.

CHAPTER 3

"I'm guessing you heard about it then?" Frasier asked, sitting on the street corner as I floated by.

I turned back and looked down at the homeless man. "Heard about what?"

"Look for yourself," he murmured, raising his hand and gesturing towards the mountain. His hand moved as if gravity acted with more force on him than everyone else.

My eyes followed as Frasier unfolded a long, knobbly finger that pointed towards the hulking mound. A streak of lightning emblazoned the spine of a book he clutched in between his left elbow and rib cage. I looked up towards the mountain but could see nothing more noteworthy than a very large heap of black earth.

"Hey man, there's nothing there."

"Look closer…", his words became shorter and sharper at my nonchalance, "…and listen."

I stood in the dead of night and noticed the

rumblings of the Earth. Growls reverberated in the depths of its bowels, like a sleeping giant tossing in its sleep.

"Look! Can you see? Can you see what is happening beneath the surface?"

I kept at it, squeezing my eyes to pierce the sediment hanging in the air. I could not say where I was, nor how I got there but the place felt strangely familiar, as though I had been there many times before. Only I had not. Even Frasier seemed to be someone I knew. His clean, robe-like garb was held to his frail body by a black rope with large knots at both ends. His skin was brown, smooth, and flawless but his croaky voice exposed his age. He was scentless, or at least his smell was indistinct from that of the dust and herbs in the bushes cushioning his back.

"Keep looking."

Amid the darkness there appeared a forming shape. Through a green haze, a tiny light the size of a firefly seemed to be in the centre of the mountain. Frasier's persistence was not needed to keep me transfixed. The light flickered and glowed brighter until its luminosity dazzled. Shapes formed within it. One, then two, then another and another, creating a montage of triangles and circles with bridges and links that fused pieces of a puzzle within a translucent ball. They were moving outward and inward, toward and away, all at the same time, creating the throbbing illusion of a beating heart. Frasier kept his eyes on me while I kept mine on the morphing and shifting shapes until they began to hold their form. There were sounds too, soothing tones accompanying the movement like a pod of whales, even though vibrations rippling through the ground quashed any momentary calm.

"What am I seeing, feeling?" My voice bounced between tones of bafflement and anxiety.

Frasier let my query linger as though allowing me the chance to answer my own question. But nothing came. My blankness and abject bewilderment animated the corners of his mouth with a subtle twitch. His hesitation suggested he was considering his words carefully.

"The smoke-screen…"

Bzzzz-Bzzzz. A sudden and irritating buzz interrupted him.

"What is this, Frasier? What are you trying to show me?" I asked again. But nothing intelligible came.

Frasier's voice faded amid the static-like noise of

a bad phone line. His body began to change before my eyes, dissolving into the undergrowth that propped him up and assimilating with the surroundings the way an amoeba might consume a smaller organism.

"Frasier!"

Bzzzz-Bzzzz.

What is that nuisance sound! I thought.

"What the fuck is going on, Frasier?"

Still nothing.

I opened my eyes and found I was back in my room, right where I was when I spoke to mum. My palms were outstretched, clutching billows of dust and reaching toward the ceiling above my old bed. In clouds, there they were again; Sasha, Dante and Eli, their faces etched by a joyous hand, a loving hand.

The pest that was my mobile buzzed and buzzed until it dragged me reluctantly from my slumber, even while in its useless 'do not disturb' mode. *One day I would summon the courage to turn the damn thing off.* Frasier's riddle woke me with a real hunger for answers. *Smoke screen?* The phone was plugged into the socket behind my wooden bedhead, giving just enough cable length to wrap around the old side table and rest on the floor an arm's length away. Lying with the left half of my face pushed into the mattress, I peeped through my right eye at the screen to see that I overslept, again. The compound effect of annoyances ended when I saw a series of missed calls. It was the company.

"Leo, are you coming in today?" a text read. My colleagues wondered where I was. They were less worried about me than they were about having to pick up my work. Screw them anyway.

"Still sick, hope to be back soon. L." I responded.

The importance of my day job was shrinking. A concoction of apathy and first world laziness fuelled my disinterest. But it was countered by my meeting with Frasier the night before. Encountering him was paralysing, sure, but it was just the spark that ignited my curiosity enough to get out of bed and push me into a new—even if unknown—direction. Sasha was gone, so the dominating questions in my mind became: *smokescreen? What smokescreen?*

That dream marked the very beginning of a series of experiences that straddled the boundary between sleep and wake. The boundary was often difficult to pinpoint, like the distinction between each colour of the rainbow. In addition—not that I believed in fate— this man Frasier, half-hobo half-wise man, invoked flashbacks of the morning at the Royal Botanical with such expressions as 'look beneath the surface'. Somewhere down in my hidden parts, prowling in the shadow of my king of hopes, I felt that this path would lead me back to my family.

Coincidentally, or not, my mother had been encouraging me to become a citizen researcher ever since Sasha left. She felt that it would be good for me to focus on some of the significant but often ignored sub-surface activity. Call it destiny, chance—call it whatever—these happenings spurred me on.

So this ambitious work to create the world's first detailed database of sub-surface activity became much worthier of my attention than my day job.

Not to mention Dr Ana Del Hoy, who led the Philomena Seismic Research Faculty.

CHAPTER 4

Dr Ana Del Hoy was stunning and reminded me of what aspiration felt like. Ana wanted to change the world. She was no ordinary scientist, and she knew it. Her voice was as soft as silk but backed up by a steely conviction that was not obvious at first. She was dispassionate to the point of aloofness. Ana exemplified the saying 'treat 'em mean, keep 'em keen'. I think it was less to do with her scientific background and more to do with the fact that she was from colder climes. Plus, English was not her mother tongue.

We met through Dave, an old work colleague of mine who did some work with the University of Philomena in the past. When Sasha left, he insisted that I find myself a distraction that would be 'in my league'. The Professor—as I affectionately called her sometimes—had an intriguing nature and cared a lot about her work. Having relocated from mainland Leidenturia to this English-speaking corner of Amplaviridi, she epitomised commitment and curiosity. For a specialist in Geophysics, the Republic of Divitia was a land of opportunity due to its significant resources and opportunities to research natural phenomena.

Many people thought she was a bit goofy. Clever, yes, but not totally there. She presented herself as a straightforward, open person yet even I saw there was something missing. There was an emptiness to her— something unexpressed that cast a shadow on her otherwise perfectness. I wanted to figure this out, I do not know why, but I did. She was, perhaps, the only part of this puzzle that was compelling enough to try to solve.

When I woke that June morning after meeting Frasier, I had just enough time to make it to my midday meeting with Ana. Our home was tucked away in a quiet corner of Eastmoor, where I captured data for Citizen Science and uploaded it via a university app. I took my usual route down the hill behind our home, followed by a sharp left in front of the local bakery, where wafts of coconut rolls comforted like a warm blanket. With over thirty-three years of practice under my belt, I could easily walk the route with my eyes closed.

"Eh, Leo," greeted Len from down the hill. "Why you so late?"

"Late for what, Len?" My throat tightened with irritation at his presumptuousness.

"Any news?" he enquired.

"Nothing you probably don't know already." Len loved rumours, even spreading some about me during my childhood, when he told neighbours that I saw the duppies too. But that was an age ago. "And anyway, when will you find something worthwhile to do?"

A voice in my head said *well, that was a pointless question.* Len took that as his job; poking his nose into everyone else's affairs. That was except, of course, when he was arguing with the duppies himself.

"You heard about what happened to de family down de hill?" he shouted behind me. "They been tellin' me its sumting to do with Killaby."

"Ahh, another one of your visions? Or just another one of your incoherent proclamations from beyond?" I kept walking.

Birds chirped away on Len's thatched roof which stood out among the ceramic roof tiles of the surrounding houses. The pale pink hue adorning the rest of the two-story homes around the heights withstood the sun far better than the sea of galvanised roofs at the foot of the hill.

"Wha' you doin' here anyway? More secrets fuh me?"

I turned to give Len a stern look, but his question was not aimed at me. I figured he was entertaining himself with his invisible companions.

The roads narrowed as I got closer to the parade. You could feel heat from the walls of the hut-sized buildings closing in. Fragrant aromas floated out from behind the street food vendors' stalls, luring even those with the most sated appetites. It was a welcomed smell over the drainage vapours that sat sandwiched between the bakery and the parade like a thin slice of putrid meat. Katia's stall was tucked between the furniture store and the arcade, serving the best iced coffee for miles around.

"Small black?" Katia mimed to me as I approached.

I smiled and gave a nod of approval, never disappointed by her ability to take thoughts right out of my head. My eyes glowed.

"How are you today, mister? Have you heard from Sasha yet?"

"Surviving Katia, surviving..." I said with a dry

timbre, "…you know how it is." I passed her $2.

I imagined her reply; *that smile fools no-one, especially not me. I read total strangers as easy as you like your eggs, so it is far easier to read you.*

But she was much gentler in reality, "Well, it is survival of the fittest after all, so it doesn't sound like you're doing too badly."

The understated nature of Katia's emotional intelligence made it unsurprising that she ignored the fact that I did not answer the second part of her question—the part about Sasha. Instead, she smiled from the eyes, gave me the coffee and 20 cents change. I looked downwards and then I turned to go.

"Thanks Katia, see you soon," I stopped mid-turn and looked at her one more time, "say hi to Kevin for me, won't you?"

On my way through the parade, thoughts of me and Katia came and went. It was another one of those 'what if' questions that arose when I encountered women I knew for a while, and even those I just met. The same went for those who I had seen, and those I was yet to meet.

While I appreciated her concern for me post-Sasha, I was much more grateful for the caffeine that helped to kick my thoughts into gear which, until that point, were less coherent than Lenny's declarations from beyond. The impending meeting with Dr Ana was another opportunity to catch up on some of my research and to do some more digging about the program. Her company was also a more-than-welcomed bonus of my participation.

The entrance to Philomena Campus carved a thin, long gash out of the Eastmoor perimeter. Few could afford to attend a campus of such prestige. As I entered, empty paper bags and food containers were replaced by red Hibiscus and sweet smells of lavender. Bees dived happily in and out of the bright yellow hedges. Other, less fortunate insects were crushed beneath my soles as they lay disguised in luscious blades of grass.

The weight of my thoughts pulled my head towards my feet as I watched each of my strides synchronise with another recital of what I wanted to ask Dr Ana. My time with her was precious, and a word wasted was a chance squandered. The sun occasionally flickered through the thin line of mature palm trees that covered the long walkway which granted a welcomed break from the swelter. Ahead, a sign over the large, old water fountain read: 'Welcome to Philomena'. Behind it was the reception.

"Hi, I've an appointment with Dr Ana Del Hoy at midday?"

"Are you asking or telling, sir?" replied the octogenarian behind the desk.

"I…"

"Sit," she replied with a razor-like sharpness. "She'll be right with you."

I sat at first. Then I began to pace around the reception waiting area. Gentle wisps of air from the wooden ceiling fan stopped me from overheating with impatience. The worn runner on the floor was accustomed to the marching of waiting guests and, to the stoic rug, I was much the same as anyone else.

An echo of click-clacking heels signalled Dr Ana was nearing. My heart began to pump as if I were riding up a steep hill. By the time she arrived, the thumping nearly drowned her out.

"Thanks for coming to see me again, Leo," she greeted. "How do you like the campus?"

"Well, the interior here certainly belies its reputation. I imagined the main campus in Leidenturia probably put this outpost of ours to shame."

"Yes, yes," she said politely.

I say "ours" lightly, of course, since the only person I knew who went to Philomena was my old boss. Anyway, thanks for making this time for me."

"Thank you for coming."

"The pleasure is all mine. It's certainly more impressive than the cafés of our first meetings." I smiled, failing in my effort to contain my excitement.

"This way, then," she gestured to follow, and briskly escorted me to her office down the corridor.

Curtness is not reserved for the receptionist alone, then. I thought.

Two paces behind and to her left, I kept up as best I could.

"We're just at the end here," she said. Her limp was possibly only perceptible to those who observed her as intently as I did.

I took a deep breath of the hypnotic scent of fresh flowers she left in her wake. "Taking me to your secret place, are you? It's still early days you know," I said cheekily.

"Here we are, make yourself comfortable."

The office was clean but dark. The only light in Ana's office was obscured by a pile of books stacked horizontally on a peeling mahogany desk, forming a stairway to the sash window. A sweet scent of bread and ripe red apples almost overpowered an old smell of wood.

"It's applestroop."

"What is?"

"What you are smelling. I never start my day without a good dose of natural iron. So…" she inhaled deeply and paused before releasing a gush of air, "…do you have any recent insights into your observations of the subsurface activity, Leo?" She had a formal tone, but I thought I saw a glint in her eye.

"As a matter of fact, I do, Professor," I returned the favour. "But first, can you give me a little more about the genesis of this project? And, no, I don't mean the official line. I mean, look, Mount Killaby has been dormant for over a millennium. Why here? Why now?"

As the word Killaby fell from my tongue, mad Lenny flashed across my mind, followed by Frasier.

"You don't have to keep calling me professor, you know."

"I know." I said, all the while seeing Killaby in my mind's eye. An intensified suspicion began to take root presently.

A cool silence broke the exchange.

"So, what do you want to know, precisely?"

Smoke screen. The Truth. Sub-surface activity. These words morphed into images, which strobed across an imaginary screen as I sat back. Another flash came—the screaming man in a sorry pile of goo back at the Royal Botanical.

"Well, as exciting as it is to be a Citizen Scientist, I feel there is something that we aren't being told, in fact, I *know* there is."

I looked deep into her eyes right there, conveying my intent but also searching for that missing element of her character.

"I'll tell you what, Leo, you bring me some decent data back on that app and then, maybe, we can talk some more. Okay?"

"Over a coffee?"

"I only drink coffee if it's in a Martini." Dr Ana shot up from the chair and left the room, her mood somewhere between annoyance and sexual frustration.

The meeting was shorter than I would have liked. There were very few people or activities that took my daily life from mundane to magical like my engagement with Ana. Her impenetrable professionalism made her even more magnetising. The game—it made me feel alive. Nevertheless, it was time for me to go. My head was all over the place.

What are they hiding? What is the link between the Botanical, Frasier and this program? And what on Earth is it about Dr Ana that made it so I can't get her out of my mind?

I made my way back to the parade with these questions on an endless loop.

CHAPTER 5

"Get out the fucking way!" A van driver yelled out, dodging me in the street. Road rage was a term invented because of Divitians, I think.

I ambled back towards home, oblivious to any sounds outside of my own head noise. Katia's coffee that morning had put just enough wind in my sails to get me through that meeting with Ana. The steady rumble of traffic building on the parade with the lunchtime crowds provided a bass tone, while hunger rhythms rumbled in my stomach. Jesse's Café on the parade was always my first choice for a light lunch, since most of the other food vendors had long queues, but what Jesse lost in slow service, he made up for with ample seating and staff. He was known for rushing nothing. His napkins and wall panels were adorned with his own words—'the best things take time'."

I entered the café and sat in the far corner with my back to the open restaurant, wary that if Veronica were on shift, I would get her attention. Even if the kind of attention I did get was mixed.

"So, what's it going to be, then?" she blurted as she appeared from nowhere

"Mixed leaf and mango salad with walnuts will do me fine, if that's okay?" I said, staring into the grain of the tabletop.

"Are you going to look at me, or does the cat have your eyeballs too?"

Our glances touched with reluctance. Her thin, white polo shirt hugged her thick frame, leaving her just enough room to breathe. The black apron protected her modesty from the front, but it pushed on her chest, spilling her breast out the top and sides. She stood akimbo, forearms shimmering under the warm spotlight above my table, with a vexatious look on her face that conflicted with the desire in her eyes.

"So, no fish with your salad? Wow, you *are* changing. Whatever next? Answer my messages, maybe?" She tried to disguise her rolling eyes as she turned away.

"Thank you, Veronica," I said to her back, trying to keep the pleasantries pleasant.

Just as suddenly as Veronica appeared, I felt a light

touch on my shoulder which turned into a tight grip, then a firm pat on the back.

"This is the last place I thought I'd find you, man," said Jamal. "Keeping things civil with her, I hope."

I hesitated to find the appropriate response. The clinking and crashing sounds from the kitchen and the murmur of waiting diners dampened the effect of the awkward silence. I eventually mustered the manners to speak.

"It's not a struggle for me to be honest. That ship has long sailed. She can't trigger me like she used to, bro, despite her efforts. Besides, it's Ana I want now. And answers…"

"…yes, I see that you've been busy, or as you say, you prefer the company of a lady who doesn't bounce around the line between angel and bitch like Veronica."

"Bro, whichever side I get from her, you can guarantee it will be memorable," I replied.

I took a sip of the table water, reflecting on—that all the lessons I'd learnt from my brushes with women, one message was most clear: this was a world of duality. Not even the super bright spotlight shining down on my head could illuminate people from my past for whom even inane situations could bring out such extremes in personality the way it did with Veronica. Anyway, Jay was there now, so my parting thought was that it was better to cut her off than to be caught in that never-ending dance between seduction and frustration.

"What brings you here, then Jay?" I said, with a voice still in the doldrums.

"I should be asking you that question. You back on good terms with Veronica? Anyway, where've you been, man? And how's work?" His tone was soft, but his litany of questions reflected his concern—and relief—to see me.

"I'm good. You good?" I said, behind a half grin, half grimace.

J continued to probe, asking about me, about Citizen Science, and that he was wondering what progress I had made.

"I'm not interested in all that data stuff," I told him. "I'm much more interested in finding out what's really going on." And of course, I told him about the hot Professor.

"Still trying to distract yourself, huh?"

"I'm a single man in his prime. Life must go on."

Jamal smiled.

I was about to tell him just why I was so suspicious

about the program, but I did not think he would get it. I had never spoken to him about my dreams. The idea of meeting Frasier in my sleep would probably freak him out, and definitely exacerbate his concern for me and, as I was sure he was thinking, my paranoia and failing emotional health.

"Well bro, you gotta do what you gotta do. But don't think you can run from yourself forever."

"Go on JT, say it then, I know you want to say something," I demanded.

My attitude to him was a real departure from the past. I mean, Jamal and I went back a long way. Our bond began back in primary school when we won the three-legged race at the sports day. Neither of us were particularly fast runners on our own but tied to each other at the ankle—we were unassailable. There was a natural symmetry between us. That seamlessness extended to our friendship too and showed up in our easy conversational style the way we understood each other and came to each other's defence. Always in step from then on, J was not accustomed to me being so diffident.

I could always rely on Jamal for advice—his upbringing instilled in him a worldly wisdom. J's father Curtis Tsepiso was like a dad to me too. From the Kingdom of Makhzwane, the land-locked state in the middle of South Almeran, Uncle Curtis put steel into his character. Makhzwane was free compared with the apartheid-ridden South. His dad was one of the most influential men in my life. His mother was from a small island ten thousand miles away called Benbecland, just off the northwest coast of Leidenturia with a population of fewer than two thousand. But it was in the magical capital of Iverlochland that Jamal's parents found love.

J's dad Curtis was a great storyteller and when we were growing up, he relished the opportunity to recount the day he met his Leidenturian bride. Jamal's father was holidaying in Iverlochland with his large royal entourage in tow.

He saw her in a queue, walked right up to her and said, 'Have you ever experienced the enthralling beauty of the Kingdom of Makhzwane?'

She was taken aback by his forwardness, but he knew he just had to take his chance. Who, what or where was Makhzwane, was beyond J's mum. Uncle Curtis held his stomach and bellowed with the most clamorous laughter re-enacting his fledgling romance.

Sometimes in the most unusual circumstances, the least likely of places and when you least expect it, you find love. True love.

Jamal's dad must have told that story a thousand times, but he laughed just as heartily each time. Having moved to The Republic of Divitia in the 1970s to exploit the mining opportunities here, Jamal's parents settled down into a new life and gave birth to him a few years later. It was a new, normal life for J's dad since his royal status had no credence in Divitia. It was a bittersweet story really because Jamal's mother had been dead for over seventeen years. Sadly, she ended up taking her own life when we were teenagers. Uncle Curtis—his adoration of his wife, how he put his family above all else, even his romanticism—left an indelible mark on me.

As kids, J and I would spend our summer holidays frolicking by the river, stealing fruits from the neighbours' gardens, catching lizards and snakes, or making mini bows and arrows from the leaves of coconut trees. Once, when our parents were at work, we took the folding futon mattress out into the garden and placed it at the end of my dad's garage. The single-story structure was flat and just long enough for us to take a running jump off the roof. The stupid idea was to soar through the air at speed and land on the futon placed at the rear. After each jump we would egg each other on to see who could go higher. I went, then J, then I, and on and on it went.

Whoosh! I stretched my arms to the sky, flying as if propelled from the clutches of a sling, landing squarely onto the thick dense cushion below. I recoiled out of sheer adrenaline and sprinted back for another jump. The routine never got stale. I jumped again and, before I could get to the roof for another, J screamed a scream as if his marrow was being extracted. The horrible tone of his voice echoed around the neighbourhood, scaring even the birds from their perches. The poor twit landed perfectly in-between two cushions and snapped his right leg in two. I picked him up, took him into the house and called one of the neighbours who, fortunately for us, happened to be a nurse.

Supposedly, time is the healer of all things. Despite a very bad fracture and a stern telling-off from our parents, we carried on doing what boys do. And he carried on getting injured. His often self-inflicted injuries came in quick succession throughout our lives and I could never tell if it was solely due to his bad choices, or due to bad karma. It confounds natural order that J—prone to such miscalculations all his youth—should be bestowing wisdom upon me in adulthood.

"There's only one thing on my mind right now, J." I nodded in the direction of the kitchen. If ever someone needed a sparring partner to refine their skills against a master of deflection, I was your guy.

"You're definitely hungry for something, Leo."

"A hungry man is an angry man. Surely you remember what happened last time?"

"When you hit that guy for knocking my food out of my hand outside of the late-night takeaway?"

"Exactly."

We chuckled.

The tuna steaks sizzling on Jesse's grill spread a smell, blended hints of fresh lemon and fresh green seasoning, throughout the café. The occasional whiff of Veronica's perfume danced around me.

"Here you go, handsome," Veronica said, putting my plate down in front of me.

Her attitude was warming, epitomising the rollercoaster ride I was glad to have left behind when we split up.

"It looks great, th-thanks."

"You couldn't be more monotonic if you tried, brother," said J.

"Just trying not to feed the trolls."

J took a deep breath. "Umm, me and the boys are gonna grab some drinks tonight, you in? You could do with some downtime."

"How is downtime going to help me?" I snapped in frustration. "Your insistence on telling me how to live my life is grating, man. Can't you see I'm rebuilding? This takes focus. I need to be moving forward, making moves, not chilling out and wasting my time."

"Okay, well, let me know if you change your mind," he said while getting up from the table. "We'll be down at Tony's Rum Shack from 7, and you know what happens at Tony's." J pursed his lips mischievously, trying but failing to replace a smirk with a scowl. Even so, I could not take his glowers seriously.

J turned and disappeared into the crowds outside.

CHAPTER 6

"Drink! Drink! Drink! Drink!"

Chants echoed out from the corner of the old wooden shack. Thursday was the new Friday all over Divitia. Except in Tony's rum shack, every day was Friday. Situated downtown near the political district, the Shack stood out amongst the modern glass buildings and architectural gems. It had the character of an old man steeped in knowledge who kept it all to himself. The Shack held sentimental value to its patrons. It was one of the few buildings that had not been demolished over the years of redevelopment after the 'Coup of Coups'. I sat with my back to the door, staring at the photos of the Cultural Aristocrats that adorned the shack wall while I waited for Jamal and the crew to arrive.

"If only walls could talk, am I right?" J put his hand on my shoulder, greeting me in his usual stalker-like way. "I hope that's not the bad shoulder."

I cracked a little smile and downed my single malt.

"Look boys! Look who's decided to join us." J looked around and pointed to the back of my head. "And he's early!"

My friends laughed and jostled their way toward me. I turned to face them, putting my 'normal' act on as best I could.

Kevin stepped forward, "First round's on me then! What your poison, Leo?"

"Whiskey straight up'll do the job, Kevin!" I feigned enthusiasm. Being there by my own choice, I felt I should at least try to involve myself.

"Of course, I expect nothing less from a man of your calibre," Xavier squeaked, extending his arm from behind Kevin for a fist-bump. "When I heard there was a chance you might be coming out tonight, I dropped everything."

Xavier spoke in a way that matched his flimsy frame. Accountants were generally introverted people. A kind-hearted guy, with empathic qualities to a fault, he was probably the most eligible bachelor in the whole of Divitia.

We made our way to a table in the opposite corner of the rectangular bar under the watchful gaze of Tony, the owner. I told them I was doing fine, that work was fine, and that the horizon looked promising for me. I told them I was forging ahead with rebuilding my life and trying to figure stuff out. They seemed to all exhale at the same time and looked at each other knowingly.

He was sitting next to Dennis, who everyone relied on to bring the energy. He was the friend that always had a pun to make about a section of society, whether it was single mothers, homeless people, foreigners or whatever was current. When nothing major was happening in the press, he would pull ridiculous subject matter out of thin air. Denis was in a long, loveless relationship and spent sixty percent of his time eating, the rest of it boozing up. One thing you could guarantee was that he could make you laugh. But this time was different. his chubby face grew long and beset with worry.

"Figure what out?" they asked, almost in unison.

Well, Xavier was the only one who asked verbally. The others asked by facial expression. The kind where the skin between their eyebrows creased and stiffened and the eyelids tightened up.

"For starters, what's the deal with this Citizen Science bullshit? You heard about that, right?" I played along, even though it was obvious they had been talking about me in my absence.

"Citizen Science? Who hasn't heard about it, dude, but…" Xavier began.

"…but you're the only one I know who's so obsessed with it," Dennis butted in, shouting over everyone else.

I looked at Den, thinking what an idiot he could be at times.

"Den, calm yourself bro," Kevin said.

A weird standoff descended for what felt like minutes but was more like a split second.

"Cheers Kev!" I said as I raised my glass. I could muster no adequate response to their questions or remarks. They cared as much for Citizen Science as I cared to talk about Sasha.

"Cheers Leo, I've been fairly good. Katia mentioned she saw you yesterday?" Kev replied.

"Uh-huh." I said, in between sips. My veneer of normalcy had already broken. I deflected again, "So, did you get things sorted with your son?"

"Things are cool. Katia looks after me. But no, things aren't sorted. He still can't sleep at night and, to be honest, I know how that feels."

"What's this?" Den asked with one eyebrow raised.

It was a welcomed interjection.

Kev took a gulp of air and swallowed slowly, "We th-think it's the dreams he's been having," he replied. "They've been causing him, well… problems."

Another weird spilt second silence came in.

"Anyway, other than that, everyone is doing fine." Kev's voice dropped off a cliff.

"No, no, tell us more, Kev. What's going on?" I stirred the mischief pot a little. I was happy to stay in the shadows, giving Kev a taste of the spotlight he was just as keen as I to avoid.

Dennis and Xavier looked at each other knowingly again. My head tilted downwards as I began to question myself. *Why did I even bother coming out tonight? Despite* trying, I failed to compartmentalise, and the tentacles of ambivalence reached into every area of my life.

"Bottoms up!" J raised a glass to break the seeding conflict. My face does not lie. If that were a poker game, I'd have given my hand away already.

Kevin saw it too. He lifted his elbows from the table facing me and sat back in his seat. I swirled my drink, inhaling the phenolic and flowery fusions that over-rode the mushroom-like smell of the rum shack. Dennis was already slouched over, his shoulders reaching for the table, leaving no sharp edges to his frame, round and soft like a large, partially inflated beach ball. His stomach protruded and rocked the table from time to time. There was J to my right, elegantly poised and taking everything in, speaking only when necessary. And then there was Xavier to my left.

I looked at Kevin again, seeing a perfect family life in his image. Katia was the gorgeous wife, they had happy children and he was thriving in his job. I was still keen to shine the light of questioning on him but being the rational person that he was, he could always conjure an argument as to why his life of marriage and parenthood was better than a lot of other peoples'. He relished connection, and often questioned how true his connection was with his wife. It was too good to be true. I empathised a lot with him on that one. It wasn't that his connection wasn't real—I guess it was more a question of the depth of connection, rather than one of authenticity. Still, the very deepest and purest connections he found with us, the crew.

"Look, enough of that deep stuff," Kevin said, as if he heard my thoughts. He splashed his open palm down on the empty bag of peanuts. "I'm here to get a break from all of that." He began surveying the bar.

"What would we have done over the years without this place? Good times, eh?" Den asked.

"Better memories," agreed Jamal.

"Big. L, what's this you're trying to figure out?" Xavier asked again. Xavier rarely lets things go unanswered.

With the spotlight back on me, I was glad that it was at least with a subject worth talking about. I went on to air my suspicious feelings about the research program.

"I'm telling you, boys, there's something else going on that they're hiding from us. I get the feeling that something's missing. Don't you feel the least bit uneasy? I mean, why here? Why now?"

The truth, I thought, hearing the screams of the man back at the Botanical in my head.

"A feeling? A *feeling*? Haha," Dennis bellowed. "You sound like my wife."

"He's right," Xavier said softly.

"Dude, don't over think it. Let's just get a few more drinks." Kevin replied. He stood and nodded towards our empty glasses. "Same again?"

"Sure," I replied, with a passive disinterest in the mundanity of ordinary conversation.

They talked about women, news, gossip, blah blah blah. I slid into a slump of boredom with the routine 'life' talk that began to dominate. Kevin took a trip to the bar and back. Then Xavier took his turn, buying a round of shots. Then Jamal.

J was quiet, I noticed. I supposed he was giving the bros their time with me. But I was not with them. I just drank myself into a stupor, my thoughts dominated by the program. The guys talked and talked until their voices slowed. Individual voices grew indistinct, blending like paint on an artist's palate. At least the whiskey made sure I was warm and occupied. The bevelled edges of the cold tumbler kept my agitated fingers tips busy as I tapped away at the crystal. My elbows bore the brunt of my weight as they worked to prevent me from slamming face-first into the table. The shack itself was fizzing under the careful watch of Tony and his wall of Cultural Aristocrats behind the bar. In the dark, misty room the steady hum faded.

The Rum Shack had seen its fair share of scandal and revolution. It was deep in the political district, where the big players of industry and parliament came to wheel and deal. A place where promises were made and broken, plots hatched and re-hatched, people's futures envisioned and destroyed. Some who graced the place would have preferred not to be on the cultural wall at all, for that would confirm their presence there. The shack also had its part-time customers. Those who would come to let their hair down after work or have a few drinks at one of the seven bars that made up the famous Rum Run—Divitia's famous bar crawl. Others, like us, would come down here to reminisce, catch up and talk about current successes or to whinge about work and women. There was a small picture of the ex-Prime Minister of the neighbouring island Ferdinand, John Bishop, who was assassinated shortly after the US invaded his country.

"Earth to Leo, Earth to Leo," Jamal snapped his fingers in front of my face.

"Yeah, you. Are you part of this conversation or not?" Den slurred.

In between hiccups and gasps, Dennis went on to share legends of the Aristocrats and the notorious deals that happened in the shack, including a dreadful deal done between John Bishop and the Innostanians. Divitia was a special place—it magnetised people from all over the world. When global power-players could not get into Divitia directly, they vied for influence on our doorstep.

My interest in geo-political history was minuscule by comparison to Dennis's knowledge, though I do recall my father portraying Bishop as a despot and a real stain on the conscience of the region. As the Chief Emissary for the new state of Divitia, my father frequented the Rum Shack himself during The Days of Fire. Those were terrible days that followed our liberation from Iverlochland's colonial shackles. He was known in local government circles for his sternness and discretion—perfect for covert work.

Dennis continued to speak of The Days of Fire, when many powerful entities—companies, nations and universities—schemed to get a foothold here. After the state was created, there was a transitional period where the loyalties of the neighbouring nations were not clear, sometimes not even within a nation's own borders. In the meantime, our northern neighbour, the Northern United States and the communists of Innostan—the two major world powers at the time—were fighting for dominance in the region.

"Unfortunately, for the then-Prime Minister John

Bishop, he chose the wrong side. But you know, the thing about loyalties is that they aren't always clear are they, Leo?"

I squinted at him, puzzled by the direction of his question.

"Ask Sasha what I mean."

"What did you just say? What the fuck did you just say?"

"Pfff-haha. Man-up and stop making excuses for your ex," Den gurgled into space.

The mercury in me rose to boiling, sending me headfirst into a steaming rage. I do not remember pushing the table when I jumped up but the grinding noise across the floor, and sudden lurching from the rest of the guys, caught Tony's attention. Beneath Dennis' humorous exterior were poisonous barbs, timed for maximum damage.

"Take is easy boys!" Tony had a well-honed instinct for trouble.

"Shut up!" I yelled back.

Dennis' laughs and gurgles turned my whiskey aftertaste bitter and my idle hands into determined fists. Kevin and Xavier stepped back and watched as Jamal tried to intervene. But it was pointless.

"What kind of shit hole dive is this that you're running anyway?" I screamed at Tony. "Celebrating losers like Crazy Bishop and the rest? How does this shack even stay standing? What with all the critters you and your family welcomed here over the years, gnawing their way through your floorboards on their way to hell."

"Leo…" Jamal said, struggling from behind to stop my aimless swaying. Tony was in my sights.

"This has nothing to do with you Tony. How about you get back behind that bar there, keep serving your drinks and keep your filthy fucking trap shut!"

"Woah, woah, woah, Leo, calm down big guy," Jamal said.

"What's it got to do with you, J? It's that fat fuck who needs to be sorted out." I jabbed one finger from my tightening fist towards Dennis' sweaty, incoherent face.

"Dude, he's just trying to vent the pressure cooker," Kevin backed J up.

"You can talk J, with your shitty life. Who the hell do you think you are? Telling me I need to 'let my hair down', like you're some kind of sage! Always on my case to do something, to be something else—

something better. Take a look in the mirror before you start preaching, brother."

Kevin and Xavier stared at me in disbelief, along with everyone else in the bar. I could not see their faces—the silence said it all. Tony stopped the music too, hoping to force me into shame. Dennis just stared into mid-air, unable to fix his gaze onto anything solid.

"Assholes!" insults flew freely and, as things descended into more injurious territory, other things too. It started with my drinking glass, then I took their glasses too. Empty or not. I threw them with such violence my shoulder popped, and I sent people scampering for cover when I started smashing Tony's wall of cultural aristocrats to pieces.

As delicious as Jesse's salad was, it did little to slow the alcohol pouring into my bloodstream. Though numbed by the drink-fuelled tirade, I could still feel eyes piercing me from a distance. Half of the guests had left the Shack by then, but others remained, perhaps eager to see the spectacle unfolding—to see what levels of shame a man could bring upon himself. Broken or not, I did not matter to them. I hope they enjoyed the show. Dust clouded the dark room with the stampede that I created, leaving wafts of sweat and stale perfumes drifting through the bar. Peaty whiskey trickled down shimmering walls while I continued with the desecration of the Aristocrats. Those curious enough to remain kept themselves a good distance from my projectiles.

"GET OUT OF MY PLACE AND NEVER COME BACK!" Tony screamed at the top of his voice.

I had never seen him that angry. Chances are, it was a day of firsts for both of us. Tony ran the Shack his entire adult life. It had been passed down for three generations. He maintained the unspoken rule to never call the police, since seeing law enforcement anywhere near the Shack was bad for business.

Out of nowhere, just as quickly as my rage appeared, it vanished. Initially blinded by its power, I soon saw myself again, standing full square in the middle of absurdity. I looked around the room, simmering. No one dared to look me in the eye. I looked back at the mess I had made where our table was, chair legs jutting out, only good for firewood now. But during my moment of madness, I missed Xavier and Den slipping out. J and Kevin stood at a distance, their eyebrows raised and pulled together by the tension of worry— and fear. Not fear of me, but for me.

"Cheers boys, I'll see you all soon." I raised an empty glass and called it a night. It was time for me to go.

Stumbling toward the exit over the broken picture frames from the wall, I grimaced at Bishop's photo again between my feet. I saw something for the first time. He was pictured with a strange-looking man—a figure I should have known, but I could not place him at the time. They posed grinning from ear to ear, almost laughing at me, while they sat at the foot of Mount Killaby.

CHAPTER 7

I struggled to switch off that night, but when sleep finally came, it only brought terrors.

The Earth shook, motion permeated upwards from the depths. There was no better time to record observations for the Citizen Science program—so my assistants said, anyway. The vibrations below were the most intense they had been since my involvement in the project. To begin with, I did not know where I was. My corridor walls did not stay their usual white; their colours changed with the sky. The shifting of dazzling blues, soft oranges and deep pinks were the only indication of the passing time. Apart from that, time seemed not to exist. One moment blurred into the next, one scene into the other, as I worked on the program. My room was not my room either. I mean, it had the same dimensions, but I did not remember its transformation into a data hub. Everyday activities such as waking, eating, brushing my teeth, or checking in with friends did not feature at all. I just took observations for the program, over and over again. The only evidence of ordinary life was my favourite coffee mug that Eli made me when he was at nursery school. It steamed with my much-needed Divitian Roast as I tried to ignore the assistants that I felt were imposed on me. There was a large desk where my bed used to be, decorated with notebooks, devices, and reams of reference material.

"What can we do to assist you, Leo?" asked one of the three assistants standing behind me.

I swivelled in my chair to look at them. "Nothing," I said to the male. "I think I've got what I need. I'll be sure to let you know if I do need anything."

He had one of those faceless types of faces. The kind where as soon as you stop looking, you forget what they looked like.

"Leo, look deeper. You mustn't let this opportunity pass you by," he prodded.

"Who are you people, and what the hell do you want from me? I swear you are like a stone in my shoe."

One man and two women—they were just there, in my space, making themselves a nuisance. I could have asked them to leave—after all they were in my house— but I felt powerless to do so.

I took a slow breath in and out. "What is it that you want?"

They did not answer. Instead, they stared at me as I stared at my screen. One of the women held a book just like Frasier's, with a streak of light embossed on the spine. I could see this one up close and noted that there were no words at all on the outside. My shoulders ached for the assistant holding it; it seemed to be heavier than she was. The sun reflected off her wispy white hair, which blended perfectly with her skin. She was at least half the size of the other two. The others stood around six feet tall and darker in complexion. The man had long neat dreadlocks and milk chocolate skin, the woman was bald, and jet black.

"You say that you are here to help, but I don't see how," I said in my futile attempt to disperse them.

"We are your assistants, Leo, nothing more. Tell us, what you see. Anything?"

I let out a breath warmed by frustration, half-sigh, half-groan. I held my coffee close, my left hand tightened around the three stickmen playing football that Eli painted onto the cup. Everything else he tried to paint was undecipherable, but I knew what he meant. Illegibility does not stop the heart from knowing. It was

Eli saying: 'Daddy, I love you so much'. Raising the cup, my eyes met with the three stickmen, imagining Eli's tiny hand painting them on. Just then my throat constricted, as though a lump was growing in the oesophagus. The assistants watched on while my eyes quivered. My nose bridge probably looked like a long, narrow island in the middle of a river about to burst its banks. In my right hand, some app readings were almost off the scale. Something is happening, I thought.

"It is time," said the flimsy one to the others, seemingly in my thoughts.

Everything started to tremble. The shaking first got the tiles chattering on the roof. Some fell and smashed on the concrete steps outside the window. One or two falling would have been enough to send stray cats darting for their lives, but Eastmoor had thousands of houses. The sound of homes shattering all at once disturbed me at the deepest level. If one could feel something deep in their soul, I imagined it would be like this.

Cows and sheep scampered through the streets, dragging their iron tethers behind them in a blind panic. Lambs wailed in the stampede as they scattered, adding to the chaos. Screaming babies and small children in the distance were barely disguised by the creaking metallic yelps that escaped from the corners of buildings and lamps posts and the dull loud cracking of rock in the ground.

"Outside, now!" I yelled to the assistants as I dashed for the exit.

Again, nothing.

"Run!" I hollered again, looking back to see if they would follow. Their unflappability made me doubt that they were able to sense danger. When I looked back for the final time, my assistants were no longer there. They disappeared, just like Frasier did -literally vanishing into thin air. The whole village shook with the quake, rippling through the old and new structures alike, throwing everything around like baby goldfish in a giant bowl. My house stood on the corner of two saints, Saint Killaby Street and San Trent. Looking up Saint Killaby Street towards the mountain, I saw that Mount Killaby itself gaped.

Keep looking, Leo, look deeper. The assistants' words came in my head.

"It's all a smoke-screen," their voices emanated from nowhere and everywhere at once, echoing and over-powering the havoc. I saw their voices too,

appearing as a thick layer of mist around me.

Looking up Saint Killaby Street at the mountain, the small light in the centre reappeared, with the shapes popping out like bubbles from a simmering soup. One after the other, they formed and conjoined until I saw the sphere again, a ball of light that jumped right out of the mountain and rolled down the street straight towards me. I heard those soothing sounds again—harmonious, with a familial drawl. It was getting louder and louder. All of the urges that you get when you want to run for your life came up, but the action did not follow. Whatever power I had left—to do anything—was gone.

CHAPTER 8

I woke to an awful, thumping headache and the deafening ring of silence. Little drops of blood moistened the cracks in my lips while my heart rivalled the wingbeat of a Divitian hummingbird. Normally, thoughts come rushing to my head, but this time only the pain of my bursting bladder flooded in. My knees and hips cracked and snapped into place when I got up and made for the toilet to relieve my body of the dark yellow poison. The night before was a mosaic of blurred images, though I remembered being frozen in my body.

In the bathroom mirror I saw blood-red eyes staring back at me. They felt slightly warmer than the rest of my face and a little sore, but they glowed like embers. Their bags were the size of quail eggs which made blinking effortful, and the grey hairs in my stubble appeared to be growing faster than the black ones, scraping my cheese grater lips.

Ugh. What on Earth happened to you? I asked myself, pressing my right eye to prevent what felt like an imminent eyeball explosion.

Go back to bed, you look like shit, said the man in the mirror.

I obeyed. Stumbling back to the safety of my bed, my phone glowed by the bedside. It was Jamal and Kevin:

"Hope you got home okay last night. Let me know when you get this. J."

"Dude you were completely out of it last night. Remind me next time not to take you anywhere where there are actual people! Rest your sore head and I'll catch you later. Kev."

"Morning Big L. What's going on? You up yet? Call me. J."

There were a few missed calls from Jamal too. As the candle flickered beside a picture of the kids in the corner of my room, flashbacks from the Rum Shack danced a shadowy dance. I dropped my phone and lay immobilised trying to remember the night before.

Confusion grew. I could not understand why Kevin or J did not mention anything about the earthquake in their messages. Twilight states were described to me as beautiful things, yet this was a dark, stuck space from which I could not differentiate realities. Despite my penchant for rational thought—and trust in it to yield answers—few things exhausted me more than this desire to explain the inexplicable. For the first time, I opened up my mind to the possibility that I had been dreaming. It was even more surprising that my dreams had returned since childhood.

My childhood was full of dreams. Not dreams in the hopes-for-the-future-sense, but dreams in my sleep. Telling the difference between sleep and wake was difficult and confusing, which caused a lot of concern at school—my teachers feared for my state of mind. That was when the nail biting started. That did no good for me and the rumours spread by the duppy man, mad Lenny.

My mother, however, had no such worry. She comforted me and told me that dreams were more reality than not, while counselling me learning to distinguish the difference was essential if I wanted to avoid ridicule. It is equally important, she told me, to listen to, and understand them. They can be reflections, or they can be instructions. I never considered that all people had vivid dreams. I started to believe the lie that I was special. My mother never told me that, I just assumed.

Once, I dreamt that I visited the surviving relatives of Deane, one of my dead school friends. After his lungs collapsed, he died and repeatedly came to me in my dreams, pleading with me to persuade his family to let him go. This happened again later, with other friends who died. Sometimes they wanted me to comfort their surviving relatives, other times it was just to keep an eye on them.

On other occasions, the most powerful dreams would jolt me into action. Like if someone close to me was in danger of dying in real life, I would dream about them dying and then when I woke, I would intervene to prevent it, as I did with my old colleague, Paul. Once I dreamt that he tumbled off the side of a mountain in a jeep with his friends. I jumped out of my sleep in a cold sweat at the time. Paul was not into dreams or anything "woo-woo" like that, but I contacted him straight away and told him anyway—even at the risk of being ridiculed. He told me that he had planned to go into the mountains that weekend with his friends in a 4 x 4. He thanked me and cancelled the excursion after we spoke.

Life went on. Everyday existence tends to dull the vivacity of a person's dream recall. It did to me, at least. Ten years of marriage, parenting and getting lost in pointless politics at work put my dreams far out of reach. Only then, when the Citizen Science program was taking over our land, did my dreams return.

So, I lay there in my lavender bed sheets, tainted by a stale whiskey-sweat, and allowed my mind to shift gears, into logical thought. I was beginning to come to terms with the fact that I was dreaming. These dreams were of a different order, and their unenchanted return proved much more consequential than ever before.

CHAPTER 9

The postman knocked at the door. I glanced down between my feet at the bottom of the bed towards the chest of drawers, searching for the motivation to get up. There was Sasha's dusty letter staring back at me. It was crumpled, stained but I still had not binned it. I do not know why I kept hold of it.

The postman's knocks grew louder and faster. He came with a letter from the office. They wanted to know when I would be back to work, and then if I was okay—in that order. For twelve years I had been working for the Royal Mining Corporation, one of the largest corporations in Amplaviridi. RMC was more than just a mining business—mining was more of a legacy. About half of its $10bn of annual revenue came from its commercial real estate, another thirty percent from its knowledge consultancy arm and the remaining twenty percent from its retailing. I started in retailing. My strategy was just to get onto the payroll of the best-paying company in the region, not for its own sake, but mainly to satisfy Sasha's lifestyle tastes. I would have climbed mountains to give her what she wanted.

In the beginning, the RMC was good to me. It is reputable even now, taking into account its dubious past of human exploitation and forced labour in the mines. My induction into the organisation was the key that opened the door to my new life.

When the chairman Sir Ralph Biggleson came to say hello to his newcomers, his charm proved his most powerful weapon. "Just call me Ralph," he would often say in his rich, silky voice to the army of star-struck staff competing for his attention. Ralph was one of the titans of industry and beyond the RMC, his business ventures touched almost every industry in Divitia. He was an adored national icon who inspired many entrepreneurs over his 40 years in business leadership.

Ralph went to the University of Philomena in Leidenturia and, along with some of the rich and most influential men in Divitia, was rumoured to be a member of the secretive Hermetic Order of Illumined Brethren. No one really knew for sure. One thing was clear—if the Brethren did exist, they were the true beneficiaries of the Days of Fire. Aggressive business acquisitions took place under the smoke of regime change and helped to accelerate the concentration of power among their membership.

My job was the last thing on my mind. Five years into the role I was the RMC's leading retail expert. I had been married to Sash for about the same time. Her homely embrace protected me from the gales of financial change sweeping the Divitian economy. Corruption, mismanagement, and a good dose of national karma dragged more and more people into poverty. Being insulated from the brutal reality of job cuts and money woes was just the start of my good fortune; first, I got a promotion to the real estate arm of the business then I ascended to a strategic role in the knowledge consultancy. Yet the sun sets on even the best days.

I found myself back in bed after retrieving the letter from the postman. In my war with apathy, this battle was lost. I would have gladly festered there for days had it not been for more knocking at the door. Shouting coming from outside was drowned out by the sweat in my pillow that I held tightly over my face. Powerful dreams made me cry, or sweat—or both—depending on the pain.

"Leo! Still not answering your phone, huh? I know you're in there. I can stay out here all day, bro."

J was as persistent as a parched mosquito.

"Leo, no one's heard from you at all. Come on man. What about your job?"

"You're worse Xavier, man!" I said into the duck down in my pillow.

"…but much more equable." I imagined his reply.

After knocking in vain a few times, he moved outside my bedroom window, to avoid the gathering rain. I slid the window open and peered down at J. He managed to stay mostly dry in all that time waiting, discounting the droplets that Grandfather released from his foliage. Only a statue would have more patience.

A cool damp breeze brushed my face and, as it warmed up, the smell of rotting breadfruit arrived with the rising water vapour.

"J," a croak escaped my parched throat, "what's up?"

J smiled. "I think you know the answer to that."

Outwardly I did not flinch even a hair's breadth, but inside I started to wake up a little.

"Come on bro," he continued before insisting that I get some air, saying something about getting back to work and how fortunate I was to have a secure, well-paid job.

"Fine…" I said, disguising my disdain between grinding teeth. "…I'll be down in a bit—but no talk of work."

J was loyal, but he was more like a stone in my shoe than a silver lining. Secretly, I held a small slice of appreciation buried deep inside. If it were not for his stubborn insistence on helping me, I do not know how much worse things might have become. *What is the purpose of a well-paid job if there is no one to share in its benefits?* I thought while heading to the shower. It would have been astonishing how swiftly I fell out of love with RMC, were it not so obvious that I was only there for her. After she left me, the vulgarity of RMC became clear. The department's stated aim "to grow and share in knowledge" was the outer wrapping of its true mission: the control of resources in pursuit of wealth and power, at any cost. I came to terms with the fact that I was part of the problem. I was an enabler of the illusion.

J stood outside. Twenty minutes must have felt like an age to him while I got showered and dressed. It probably helped that I already relented to his will, yet it was in these kinds of moments that his forbearance shone bright. With my body washed of rancid odours and my tetchiness diluted, I felt a little better—admitting it was a different matter.

I went downstairs to greet him. Touching fists was not enough for J. He pulled me in, clutching me firmly with his 6ft 5in frame. There were only six inches between us, but I felt much shorter. His retracted shoulders and steely spine elongated him against my curled neck and hunched over torso.

"You must have a sore head?" he enquired. "Don't worry, bro, we handled things with Tony."

"Yeah," I exhaled. "I'm sorry about that."

"It's the past. We're here now," J said, eyes glowing with the flame of quiet intent. He was a man of more than just physical stature; his character was big and deep. We set off together for Jesse's for a late lunch and a few drinks. Well, he would drink; I could not stomach another drop of alcohol.

Eastmoor changes a lot after rain. The gutters were overflowing with mucky water and contaminants that included dead snakes, plastic bottles, baby diapers and rodents. But the sun was shining, and the rain had washed the pollution out of the air, so it was good to be outside. Looking at J striding beside me, I noticed he was holding a copy of the Divitian Times. I noted the date. It was May 4th, exactly 20 years and one day since his mum died.

"Shit man. I'm so sorry, J, I didn't even check in with you and your dad. How is he?"

"20 years is a long time," J explained.

"It is."

J said he was happier than he had ever been. Until recently, Jamal had been a single man enjoying the life of a 'creative'. He hated that term though, because he felt that, in truth, everyone was creative—it was just unfortunate that some of us had forgotten. He was disciplined and efficient with his time to such precision it appeared obsessive. It just seemed that everything flowed with him.

In the last three months he found Charisse—the love of his life. It was still "early days" for them, but he described the way they connected as nothing less than magical. They fit hand in glove and their shared love for scooters—and a near-addiction to adventure—took them all over Divitia. He was right though; 20 years was a long time. I knew so many people who could never move on from loss.

He was especially close to his mother before she lost her will to live, yet the tragedy never seemed to do anything but good for his outlook on life. He always expressed his gratitude for her love and that it was better to have experienced love and loss, than to have never experienced love at all.

"Bro, the thing is, I see the truth now. I see that I have the power to choose how I respond to my feelings and which emotions I want to empower. Grief can be a destructive force if you let it consume you. Trust me. I have seen it up close. Bro…" J let a slow breath out, "…you know…"

"…I know." I cut him short.

His tone signalled the beginning of a lecture.

"Isn't it enough that I came out? I don't need a sermon as well."

"Fair enough Big L." J patted me on the back and tried to say something else.

I listened instead to the cawing crows competing for their perches in the trees, and the low hum of the bustling parade in the distance ahead. The birds flew around as if they were crazy, from branch to branch and tree to tree, forming large black patches in the sky and below. Within their shadows, the air cooled. After

J saw that pushing me was not the way, he too walked in silence.

Soon we heard the beat of the parade. The thumping music from sound stalls excited the air and drowned out the birds.

"Man, it feels good to be alive!" Jamal erupted.

He put his arm around my shoulder and smiled. Sandalwood wafted off his collar. The three-inch plait dangling from his chin was the most obvious feature of his new look. Anyone could sense the air of freedom that he radiated—it was infectious.

At 3pm the paradors transformed the street from lunchtime into a more carnivalesque evening set up. As far as Divitians were concerned, every day was a good day to party. Reggaeton rhythms bellowed out of side streets and escorted us all the way to Jesse's front door.

"Eating today, or just here to drink?" greeted Veronica.

"Who comes to Jesse's just to drink?" asked J.

"Judging from the form he's been in recently," Veronica pointed at me with her eyes, "I suggest you eat well before you booze tonight." She wore a naughty, self-satisfied smirk of a child who got away with stealing.

"Mind if we sit here?" Jamal butted in, hoping to avoid anything more inflammatory.

"You miss her, don't you?"

"Who? Veronica? Don't be stupid."

J just smiled and sat back. He knew things remained strained between Veronica and me since our fiery romance ended. She was very sexy, but I doubt she was aware of her power in that regard. Whenever I came to Jesse's she would go out back and return with fresh lipstick. She knew I loved her most in red.

When I was low and most vulnerable, Veronica was everything to me. She comforted me when I needed comfort, she was a friend when I needed to talk, and she was a lover when I wanted connection. When I was flatlining, her feminine zest was like caffeine. But Veronica wanted a lot more than I did. Starting a family was old news to me, and that simple misalignment killed any potential between us. Many things remained unsaid, particularly on my part. I do not think I really expressed to her how much I appreciated her. Our compatibility extended to many areas in life, but not all of them, and not the ones most important to her at the time. In any case, I did not know what I really wanted, but I knew that the idea of a new family evoked a suffocating feeling in me.

Jamal put the Divitian Times on the table. In the bottom left corner, it read: "Citizen Science is changing lives for good. The University of Philomena is recruiting now. Be part of history in the making, right here in Divitia. Sign up at your local superstore."

He caught me staring. "How *is* the Citizen Science project going by the way?"

"It's curiously all-encompassing, interesting and perplexing all at once."

"Equivocation never suited you."

"Uhuh, a bit like that plait on your chin?"

"Ha. Seems like they're amassing a small army for this Citizen Science thing. Interesting, huh? That so many people want to dilly-dally with all this when there are many more important things going on for us Divitians? Do you get what I'm saying, bro?"

I saw exactly where he was trying to take me with this. But I had become so adept at this game by now that I could dance around his every subtlety, side-approach, and circumnavigation—and he around mine.

"That's what I'm going to find out tomorrow at my appointment with Dr Ana. Look, J, I know you want what's good for me," I paused to let out a long, turbulent breath. "But some strange things have been happening to me and…" I stopped.

"…and?"

"…I just know…something's not right with this."

I wanted to tell J about the dream I'd had the night before, but I struggled. I was only just coming to terms with the fact I was dreaming myself. Plus, linking that getting reuniting with Sasha and the kids? I feared what he might say. There was a strong likelihood that he would blame it all on the alcohol, which was another avenue I did not want to go down.

"I'll tell you what…" J changed the subject. "…I was thinking bro, once you are back on your A-game, we could take a little holiday somewhere, somewhere different. Something different from the usual beer-fuelled city breaks we're used to taking." J put both palms down on his thighs. "I close my eyes and I can see us with our damsels, experiencing the freedom of life. The kind of freedom we always wanted but never had the courage to seek—connecting with animals, feeling the raw energy of Mother Nature and being at one with all life. You know?"

"Where's the whiskey in this equation?" I half-jested.

J laughed. We reclined into an easy flow of conversation—how it always should have been. We reminisced and talked about things we had not talked about in many months. Nothing particularly meaningful, poignant, or revolutionary –it was simply good to chat about nothing. It was the first time in a long time that I laughed. Only J had the kind of presence to impact me this way. It brought into sharp focus why he was my best friend—how he read me, how he knew how far to push and when to let up, how he could bring my burning business with Citizen Science and Philomena to a temporary halt. I was glad that he did not give up on me at my window that day. He gave me the reprieve that I needed to recharge. The energy that I needed for what was to come was unbounded.

CHAPTER 10

Ana and I exchanged a few text messages about the research the next day and, feeling reanimated, I proffered that Espresso Martini. Every communication with Ana tested my salesmanship. It might have been easier to locate Sasha and the kids and persuade them to come back than it was to gain Ana's assent. I could not place the motivations underlying my craving for her. Maybe it was her association with Citizen Science, Philomena—and hence the truth—or that she was a gateway to something else that gave her that narcotic power over me. The reasons intertwined like the braid of a fishing line hooked firmly into my mind.

Making space in the kitchen to sit, I perched beside books and old magazines, dirty crockery, and a pile of mail at the edge of my breakfast table. My coffee habit made my kitchen a prized location, but even mother would have been disappointed to see me treat any room so ungraciously. My phone jumped with a sudden vibration and, much to my delectation, it was the Professor's reply.

"Sound good," she texted back. "How about Barcello Cocktails on 33rd street, 6pm? You're buying."

I told her it would be my pleasure and that I was looking forward to it more than anything. She could not see then how my skin shimmered with the glow of satisfaction or the tiny bubbles of excitement popping in my stomach. I had met Ana a few times before, but something about that day felt different. I wanted to say more, but I could not get the words out. Excitement alone was not the cause of my random mutism, just the effect of it.

Later, I went back down the hill towards the parade to hail a cab to the venue. Torn brown paper bags and nocturnal fruit flies blew through the space the vendors vacated, leaving the taxi rank beside it stacked with idle drivers. Sand flies and mosquitoes danced around the evening sky, sending the bats into a food frenzy as sunset ushered in a new phase of activity. I headed straight into the back seat of the first cab in line.

"Barcello Cocktails." I instructed the driver as I got in.

The taxi driver squinted at me through his rearview mirror.

"Looks like date night for somebody tonight?" He leered, then paused a while in recognition, "Ah, I haven't taken one of your kin in my car since your father, son."

"Max?" I replied with surprise. I almost missed his comment, my mind stuck on Ana. "I thought you'd retired!"

"Yes, yes, still in the game, son. The Order keeps me rather busy these days. If it wasn't for your father and taking him there over the years, I would never have gotten such a loyal customer base. You know those Illumined Brethren, they only select from a tiny pool of drivers, you understand. So," Max, paused and released a long sigh, "...I keep going. It gives me something to do, you know... keeps me busy."

I soaked it in, watching his bulbous fingers slide silently on the steering wheel. "You used to take my dad to the Brethren?"

"Many times! Though he stopped suddenly one year, I've forgotten how long ago now. We called them the HOIB. Like, *Hoe-ebb*," he stressed the pronunciation.

My dad? A member of the Hermetic Order of

Illumined Brethren? I thought.

"But, Max, aren't the HOIB just legend?"

Max laughed a knowing laugh. It was not quite condescension, rather an if-you-only-knew kind of laugh that rumbled deep in his throat. He continued to talk with the enthusiasm of a grandparent at story time.

"I'm sure many of the tales you have heard are not true. I am also sure that many of them are. From what I can gather, since the Days of Fire, the HOIB has been expanding in Divitia. Membership is by invite only you see, it's a very exclusive club indeed. The things I have heard over the years…. Well, let's just say you wouldn't want to repeat them." Max's eyes took to the mirror again, reflecting his gaze like a laser beam deep into my soul. It was a momentary glance that felt timeless. "One thing sticks with me still. Now bear in mind Leo," he broke off mid-sentence, as if searching his mind for his next words, then choosing them with extra care, "I learned to never ask questions."

Max talked as if he needed company. His features hid beneath the shadow of his perma-trilby so I could not quite see him, but his voice trembled softly, in the way that only age shakes it, so I imagined his face to be deeply lined.

"Why so talkative if things were so hush-hush?"

Then he replied with further divulgence, as though my question was never asked. "I listened very closely, hoping to find out more about Killaby and why they were so interested in it. From what I can tell, there is a gateway of sorts up there—oh, I don't know—something super-natural, let's say. I could never get beyond that but believe me, I have been waiting a long time to find out."

His words penetrated the depths of my mind. But Max was not one for quiet. He kept on, asking more about my father and how he was.

"Dad's fine Max, he's enjoying a quiet life on the Southmoor Coast. He has grown used to solitude."

"Good man," said Max. "Perhaps he's writing his memoirs. The number of things your father's forgotten... it would take a few lifetimes for a mortal like me to learn."

"I hear you, Max. How about Harry, anyway? How is his wife? Has he given you any bouncing grandchildren yet?" I smiled.

My question prompted a heavy silence as Max considered his words again. "I'm afraid not, son. Harry's not been the same since things went south between him and Camille. You wouldn't recognise him now. It's like something possessed him, I suppose. It just got in and ate away at him from the inside. He told me about you too, I'm sorry to hear." His voice tailed off. It was as if the surging tide that brought his loquaciousness swept it away forthwith.

He talked less when he drove my father places when I was little. All dad's transport needs when he worked in the local government offices were met by Max, without fail. When dad found someone he could trust, he trusted them not only with his life, but with ours, mine and my 3 siblings'. I was quite sure that Max could afford the highest-spec taxi from dad's custom alone.

Creeping through the evening traffic, the buzz of Eastmoor faded with distance. My thrill at meeting Ana wiped away any remnants of my brief teetotalism. Barcello lay in the leafy outskirts of Westmoor, our wealthier neighbour. The buildings were set further back from the road than in the parade, parted by an extra-wide pavement and a thick grass verge. Some sections of the verge were raised with handmade bricks and planted with flowering plants from the rainforests of Amplaviridi. The streets were kept sparkling clean which I could see even in the night time; streetlighting was cut back after much lobbying by the Westmoorian residents committee.

"Barcello's coming up!" Max announced. "What's the celebration? What with your manly aroma and impressive outfit, I'd say whoever she is, she's very lucky indeed."

I smiled back at him in mirror, "Pleasure? Possibly. Business? Definitely. Especially after the conversation we just had, Max," I said, exiting the taxi. "Good to see you again."

Barcello's was not as busy as I expected for a weekend. The cylindrical four-story building was draped in chain-links and up-lit with purple and pink. It was probably how the 1980's architects imagined the future but when the future finally arrived, it looked more like a relic from an old sci-fi movie.

I followed the brick-paved path towards truth and opportunity. The glowing edges of the entrance gave the place a feeling of exclusivity.

"Welcome sir," a black-suited gentleman opened the door as I approached.

I thanked him with a nod and entered the lounge, the atmosphere thick with smells of cinnamon and vanilla.

I believe the pros call it 'suggestive ambience'. On my left were murmurs of intimate conversations around miniature table lamps that offered a subtle glow. Over to the right, just beyond the private booth area sat Ana, sipping something, and reviewing a file.

I approached the table. "Anything exciting?" I asked, nodding to the document.

"Oh, there you are," she said, sliding out of the booth to greet me. She stood and we shook hands, leaning forward to touch cheeks. I held mine to hers, letting it linger for a fraction longer than was typical. I wanted to smell her, yes, but I mostly wanted her to smell me—to initiate the dance between chemistry and physics, between lust and knowledge.

"Leo, I hope you don't mind that I took the liberty of ordering you an Espresso Martini while I was waiting for you to arrive. You planted the seed, and I was dying for a drink."

"I wouldn't have it any other way." I replied. "But I'm just as thirsty for some honest, reliable information," I finished, pulling out a notebook from the breast pocket of my jacket. She seemed surprised— she was normally the one to get straight to business.

"Please, ask away," she said, her eyes twinkling

with amusement.

"You asked me to come back to you with something worth discussing."

"I did."

"Well…" I started, fiddling with my unopened notebook. Then I ran out of words.

It appeared again—that pesky lump in my throat. As misaligned as Veronica and I were, she knew me well; the cat often did have my tongue, especially when it came to tricky conversations. I did not have any profound insights from my Citizen Science observations, I did not have any great breakthroughs with the data, nor did I have any good ideas to present to her. I became conscious then of how much I wanted to extract from her and how little I gave in return. I was still desperate to know the truth about their motivations, and I had to find out myself.

"What's going on in Killaby?" I spat it out like a bad taste.

"Oh, this again. But nothing for me."

"I want to know what Philomena is really doing here, who's involved and why. I've been hearing things, Ana, feeling things, about the whole program. I only got involved because I needed something stimulating to do. You know? Something worthwhile. A way to contribute to Divitia, to the region, maybe even the whole world. Then things started changing. I started to get these clues."

"Clues? Your behaviour, Leo, this constant nagging about my project, is bordering on compulsive."

I wanted to confess. Not being able to speak to anyone about my feelings and experiences and the intense dreams that I had been having was carking.

"How do you feel about dreams?" I asked. Her eyes expand with interest.

"I suppose dreams can be powerful things. Is that what you meant by clues?"

"Sort of," I said. I felt a slow depressurising inside.

"My father always believed that dreams were clues. They can reveal quite a lot. Why do you ask? Have you been dreaming about me?"

I wasn't but it didn't make her less appealing. I just still felt that prodding sensation. The invisible rod stoking the fire in me to connect the dots. So I accepted Ana's invitation to share more and I told her everything. I told her about the dream with Frasier, I told her about the helpers and the earthquake. I gave her everything else I had, leaving nothing untouched. Well, apart from Dante, Eli. I described the fiery intensity of my feelings, the appearance of odd shapes and familiar sounds and the ultimate insolubility of events. I wanted to go on, but Ana became ghost-like.

"Are you okay?" I asked.

"You're giving me chills."

Neither of us could speak then. Even though it was not a conscious decision, it felt appropriate at the time. It was merely something that happened. We did not need words anyway because the swirling of the remnants of our cocktails spoke volumes, our minds locked into the process of making sense of everything so far.

Ana raised her eyes from the glass, "Leo, can I share something with you?" She released a loud breath and adjusted her posture. "My father always guided me firmly along the academic path, but he also knew there was more. There was more to life. My mother used to call him dromenvanger, dreamcatcher to you. He was a very serious man, but he knew things. And his predilection for dreams means I can much better appreciate your motivations now." Ana drew closer and extended her open hand. "Can I feel you?"

I opened my hand. She ran her fingertips along the

lines in my palm, relaxing into thought. She started to tell me about her childhood, and how limited it was compared to her friends'. Her life was scheduled to capacity. If it was not piano, athletics or science lessons, she was in formal education.

"My parents told me I was born to be a scientist. They knew it from the moment I could speak. Perhaps it's a genetic gift! I don't know, as I never knew my biological parents. My adoptive mum is now dead, for reasons I'm still not entirely clear about. Dad just said, 'she died in an accident.' Dad practically raised me on his own, or so he would have you believe. I would say that he did a marvellous job, obviously. But he did have the help of a few nannies over the years," she chuckled.

Ana became more attractive the longer our conversation went on. It was clear that I did not know anything about her at all, other than her credentials and perhaps, judging from her clothes, that she liked turquoise. I knew Ana looked like she was in her early thirties, but I was not sure. Until that point, she hid her inner workings behind a curtain of mystery. What she lacked in inner confidence she compensated for with her sexuality—and qualifications. It worked wonders for her in the academic world. Along with my attention, she seemed to like my intellectual curiosity but if I were a betting man, I would say it was my determination that hooked her.

Ana slowly tapped her foot next to mine and started edging out of the booth.

"I love this song! Shall we dance?"

She pulled me by the hand towards the open dancefloor on the other side of the bar. The parquet flooring distinguished the dance floor from the rest of the lounge. A slow instrumental played in the background, reminding me of the sexy zouk songs I heard growing up in some of the immigrant districts around Divitia.

"Do you know how to dance to this?" She asked.

She turned around to face me, slowly starting to gyrate. "I love this!"

She pulled me closer towards her. The zouk was slow and hypnotic though I was not schooled in the undulating movements needed to dance to it, but I was confident enough with my Divitian genes. I followed her lead for a few steps and slid into my own groove, one that slotted into balance with hers.

Once our hips locked into rhythm, all sense of time

started to fade. The enduring herbal hints in her hair clung to the insides of my airway when she pressed her soft forehead against my cheekbone. Her face was red hot, but her body was cool against my chest. My body dispensed its own doses of chemicals, giving me a natural buzz that stalled every passing second, as if I could jump and watch the world rotate beneath my feet. It was as if events were under a power so great that my will was no longer my own. She too grew in intensity. I could sense it by the way she rubbed the back of my neck with her fingers and the deepening of her breath, each one she carefully brushed against my ear.

Like in a dream, the world around us began to crumble away, leaving just the two of us on a tall column of Earth, topped with parquet flooring. In the gaps when she did let me go, her hands ran down her flanks, pulling my mind to what shapes lay beneath her flowing dress.

Our eyes met for a flicker of time before our lips touched and melted into a moist expression of pure desire. As the grip of her hand tightened in my back, rhythmic urges travelled through my veins and into her soft body in front. Our clasp was firm yet fluid like a waveform dancing with its shadow. I moved to the rhythms of a deep craving to feel her closer, deeper, purer, without impediments. I could feel in her—and she in me—that unmistakable taste of looming ecstasy. Just as my lips parted, and I took her smell in with a breath, she spoke my thoughts before I could.

"Are you going to take me home tonight, Leo?" Her voice was pulsating, oozing up from far down in her body.

"What about your father, isn't he at home?" I whispered back but she danced over my words with nonchalance.

That night I learned there was a time for talking, and that was not it.

CHAPTER 11

Ana left a sultry indentation on her side of the bed the next morning, slightly dampened by her bewitching fragrance. If not for the whizzing sound of machinery coming from her kitchen, I would have remained in a twilight trance. The sound carried from the kitchen down her hallway for a few metres and reverberated outside her bedroom door like an unwanted guest—polite enough not to enter, but happy to stand outside and scream.

I could not recall a time I slept more soundly. It almost hurt to try. Still, wakefulness had to come, and it crept up on me. My morning mind beckoned a blend of thoughts and memories, helped along by the cues of crisp linen and sugary pillows. Soon the whizzing in the kitchen stopped and Ana's bare footsteps came gently thudding down the hallway. Trim as she was, her footsteps still gave her limp away to ears as well-trained as mine. She put her bum to the door, pushing back-first into the room, with loaded hands.

"Smoothie?" she asked, extending one glassful to me, "I used freshly-picked fruits."

I sat up in the bed and nodded, "I could use the boost, or I may just stay in bed all day."

"You did very well, Mr," she winked.

Ana dropped herself beside me, sending little particles bouncing off the sunbeams in the room like snowflakes. She leant over and pressed her soft lips on mine. "Drink up," she said, "I want to give you a tour of the orchard."

It was a moment to savour. I wished I could stop time, like in Barcello's, so I could dwell in that bliss. It flew by instead, much quicker than it would if I were having the best days of my life. It is a strange kind of phenomena—when you wish for something to last forever, but it disappears even faster, just to spite you.

In three silent gulps I was done and slipped out from beneath the covers to follow Ana outside. The hallway was decorated with photos of her growing up. She looked like a happy, secure child wrapped in her gorgeous mother's arms. Her mother had the jet-black hair and olive skin of Southern Leidenturians, with a glow of contentment around her. Ana's father was of a different sort. He stood tall and proud, but the photos captured an air of ugliness. His features were handsome enough by typical standards, but if you look beyond the square jaw and chiselled face, his expression suggested pain and darkness. It was in the eyes, unhidden behind his face-wide grin. Something else struck me about him, but I could not connect the dots just then.

Ana took my left hand with her right and led me through to the kitchen back door. Giving it a gentle push with her other hand, she led us out into dazzling light.

We walked down the outdoor steps, past the hammock to the driveway. Even to Divitians, those houses built into the side of mountains confused the mind the way each level seemed to be on the ground floor when you entered via one door, but then an elevated level when exiting through another.

"This is where I get my inspiration," she said, pointing at a hammock to our right and below. "I spend my time out here thinking, planning, visualising the next steps for the study. Look!" she pointed to a snake making its way across our path towards the grass, "it's a sign! My father always said that."

"A sign of what?" I asked.

"He always said to me that it was a sign of something happening in the unconscious. Not that I knew what that meant as a little girl. I mean, I barely know what it means now to be honest. I'd rather stick to simple science."

The corners of my mouth raised as if I just had a mouthful of sugar. "I wonder what is coming out from your unconscious?"

"Well, Leo," she said, with a smile exponentially sweeter than mine, "who says it's my unconscious and not yours?"

"Ha!"

Ana spoke in a new voice. Anyone else present might hear the old Ana; the doctor, the one burdened by a persona with the same timbre and intonation as before. But I was more perceptive in that moment. She dropped the character cloak—the one she needed to wear when she was busy not disappointing her father, to live up to the expectations of her peers in private school. The one who never got hurt or took anything personally.

It was a persona she wore so well and for so long, she rarely undressed, probably not even while alone.

But I saw her, the one who dwelt beneath the titles and accomplishments, beneath the upbringing and job description. Her nakedness and vulnerability showed me for who she was because, in that moment, she was not trying. Since I told her about the dream at Barcello, she began to bear herself to me, but I missed it the night before, spinning in my own whirlpool of endorphins. I failed to see her then as I did in her orchard. I wondered why I never saw Sasha this way.

"Come on then, there's more down here," Ana yanked on my arm. She proceeded to take me to the maids' quarters.

I told her how beautiful her home was, and how difficult it must have been for the groundsmen to maintain a garden on such a steep slope.

"This is Westmoor," she replied, "apart from Killaby itself, all the Divitian power lies here."

My face bent quizzically.

"It's a wealthy area, Leo, that's all I'm saying. We get the top tier service, in everything, including gardeners."

There is that Killaby again, but in my care-free state, my mind had already moved on to the side of the house towards a wrought iron gate directly below the stairs from the kitchen. I thought about Sasha as we walked, with the harsh contrast between them expanding inside me.

Ana unlocked a large combi-lock and opened the rusty gate that protected a dark corridor, granting access to laundry facilities and studio apartments. I put my foot on the step and stopped for a few seconds, feeling a chill run across my body. There was a definite shift in me, but I could not place its source.

As we entered through the archway, I noticed more picture frames like the ones upstairs. Except these frames were not housing traditional family photos, they displayed awards of some kind. Straight away I recognised the gold seals on them, which caught the little lighting there was.

The first certificate read: "To Chancellor Raymond Strachan, in recognition of his scientific research into natural phenomena". It was embossed with the lightning streak from my dreams and signed by the president of the HOIB. The chill, still making its way up my spine, turned ice cold and the atmosphere thickened.

"These are certainly impressive awards," I noted, pointing, and swallowing to disguise my suspicion. "Who is Raymond Strachan?"

"Oh yes, that's my dad. Didn't I mention that last night? He did awesome work over the years as the chancellor of Philomena. His work is central to the Philomena's research going on. So, all thanks go to him for what we're doing here! Not many have had the privilege of working with him, or even speaking with him, him being an introvert. He always loved working alone for some reason."

"But you know, I…" My face shone back at me in the frame while I looked and listened. Ana whipped her eyes across at me.

"…I know what you're thinking, strange for a chancellor, right? I know. But he managed his role somehow, despite this."

Ana thought nothing of her throwaway remark. I wanted to ask more about him, given that his presence was so dominant in the house. But Ana just wanted to move on with the tour and I was keen to avoid erasing the progress made between us.

A flicker of light caught my eye—a flash but subtler. Then a shape moved from one of the maid's apartments. I would have snapped my head across to get a good look had the temperature not slowed my reactions down so much. There was no rush because the shape was moving rather patiently.

Eventually, my eyes found the back of a figure—a man, walking quietly towards a half-height door some 10 metres away at the end of the corridor. I looked at Ana as if to ask her about what I was thinking, but it was not necessary. I remembered the photo on the wall inside, his broad shoulders and elongated neck giving him those extra few inches height on his already-stretched legs. I could not see his eyes yet, but I saw enough to know it was the Chancellor, Ana's father, Raymond Strachan.

"Come on, then," Ana said, and followed him right up to the door and stopped.

I followed with trepidation weighing down my feet. My hand began to sweat in hers. Or hers in mine, I could not tell whose was to blame. All I knew was that mine was cold. *Do I ask her to introduce me to her father?* I thought. A scintillation of doubt flowed from my voice to my limbs and put me in an awkward position.

"Go on in then, feel free to look for whatever you like. I'd better leave you to it. This is why you are here, isn't it? Go on, be my guest," Ana insisted.

She looked pleased, wearing the self-satisfied

expression of accomplishment. She was pleased, I guessed, that she was trusting someone other than herself with her records. With her father now present, I figured she felt more secure.

I stood at the open door, looking from a distance into the dark room for the chancellor. He could not have gone far. It was certainly a good chance to get the information I needed first-hand. I looked at Ana again, then at the shelves stacked with files and hard drives within.

"Where do I even start?" I asked her.

"That depends on what you are looking for, Leo. Do you even know?"

My happiness was dimmed by her question. She remained unruffled. She gave me one more glance of quiet reassurance, telling me that it would be okay to enter her basement room.

"Oh, and Leo, why not come back for dinner tomorrow so we can discuss what you find, yes? Have fun!"

She did not wait for my reply, leaving me with the last words I heard from her that day. Her strides back down the archway bounced with confidence; she knew I would be back. If not for her, then for her father.

I stooped and squinted into the darkness. There was a pungent smell of rot accompanied by a growling sound that bounced off the low ceiling. The books and shelving absorbed much of the volume but did nothing to dampen its horrifying effect.

"Mr Strachan?" I mumbled, my voice an octave higher than usual.

No reply accompanied the crunching sound of gravel underfoot. Bent over, I edged my way in, feeling for the light switch on the walls. Irregular sounds of dropping water coupled with breath-like beats of an animal panting. The room stretched back half the length of the corridor and was no wider than three or four arm's lengths. I cleared the door and stood up with my head bent forwards, just clearing the ceiling. Amid darkness, a piece of string tickled my head. I pulled on it and a dim, yellowish light came on behind me.

"Mr. Strachan?" I called again, but nothing.

I continued into the darkness. The light behind swept around my body and showed crumbling walls to my sides, leaving everything else hidden in my shadow. I moved forward and called again.

"Ray, it's a pleasure to meet you. My name is Leo. I'm part of the Citizen Science program you're running. I'd like to talk to you about your work." I tried again to no avail.

Yet I heard him move and I felt his presence. It was a game of cat and mouse that fuelled my apprehension. Nevertheless, I inched towards him in the corner. That was when I saw it.

First, I saw the eyes. They glowed red in the body of my shadow. Our eyes met before he stepped forward towards me. I wished I could run but my legs weakened, almost to collapsing, when I saw the tips of his black horns protruding from his skull. Only tiny parts of him were visible. The corpse-like smell emanating from his skin would have overcome me if fear had not taken control of my body. His ashen colour and charcoal texture spooked me backwards to the door. He said nothing on his approach. If he had, the encounter would have been even more remarkable, so desperate was I to hear the chancellor's voice at last. Even while in the grip of dread there was a feeling of familiarity—as repulsive as it was—as though I had met him before.

Pushed backwards out of the storage room, I seized my chance to run. With a swift turn, I shot down the archway, past the doors to the studio apartments, past the awards that hung in the walls and back into the brilliance of Westmoorian Heights. I was tempted to return to Ana upstairs, but I was in shock and desperately ashamed of the urine running down my legs.

I opted for home instead.

CHAPTER 12

It took me three good hours to walk back to Eastmoor. When I arrived home, I still did not feel safe. The water from the old showerhead rolled down my temples as I watched the water run off my body, waiting for the fear to drain away with it. Only in my worst nightmares had I seen such a frightening creature; never did I expect to see one in real life. I hoped desperately that a hot shower would get me back to a more stable state of mind. I felt a sudden singeing in my skull, and my mother starting to talk to me. 400-odd miles away in Ferdinand, she could have been anywhere in the world, it would not have mattered because mother communicated with me at will—her will. She was never intrusive, only reaching in when she felt concerned. There was no denying that burning sensation inside the base of my skull.

Leo, I'm picking you up, what's going on with you?"

"I don't even know where to begin," I said, shaking my head in a vain effort to dispel the images blemishing my mind.

"Start at the beginning," she replied with the calm that only a mother knew how to do.

"I've been doing the Citizen Science program as you suggested, and you were right to think I would find some answers there. It's all too much to go into in detail, but the dreams came back. And then I met this woman who is leading the Citizen Science project which has all been going fine up to now. And then these dreams, they just keep coming. These really powerful dreams, Mum, and they're all centred on Killaby…"

I broke off, blinded by a flashback that muted me for a while. I saw myself leaving Tony's Rum Shack and stepping over that photo of John Bishop on the floor. I remembered his face and the grinning man with him at the foot of Killaby. That grinning man was Raymond Strachan.

"Leo? Say something. Take your time but talk to me at least …Leo?"

I drifted off into prolonged quiescence; there was a spinning inside my skull like a fairground ride, making me sick to the stomach, then I toppled into a stew of memories. But with time, and a generous helping of mother's patience, I was able to tell her more. I went on about the smokescreen that I heard the man shouting about at the Royal Botanical, how it had stayed with me ever since.

"...the pieces of the puzzle are coming together. I'm sure now that the answers lie on Killaby. To Philomena, to Sash...to everything."

My voice tailed off. "I followed Ray into that room, mum, honestly, but when I got in there, there was a kind of...well, demon, or monster... I don't know."

My mother listened with intent. As a half-telepath, I could not see her but I could feel her. Once I was exhausted of words, mother only offered her usual; "You're doing well, son. Continue to dig and find out what lies beneath. Perhaps that man, Raymond Strachan you say? Perhaps he holds the key to your next stage. I am confident the truth awaits you, if you have the courage to face that demon again."

CHAPTER 13

Many apologies later, things with Ana returned to the way they were before I vanished from her place unannounced. I said nothing about what I saw in her basement, fearful of offending her or worse, have her think I was a lunatic. She calmed down quickly enough to keep our dinner plans in place. After my conversation with my mother, I slept off a little more of the stress that the shower could not rinse. But regardless of how many showers I took, and how many hours I slept, homeostasis eluded me.

On the taxi ride back to Westmoor, I noticed nothing outside the car except for Killaby itself. As it grew in my mind, it loomed larger toward the south. A great big backdrop darkened in the dimming light, watching over our every move. In the trunk of the car my overnight bag rattled around, packed with a change of clothes to save myself more embarrassment from any further episodes of incontinence.

When we pulled up to Ana's stately home, I thanked the taxi driver with a large tip and made for the rear to retrieve my bags. Spikes atop the gate to her home stood like glossy black bayonets held by soldiers welcoming me with a guard of honour. Its whirring sound of motorised hinges opened, revealing her snaking driveway and toward the end, I saw Ana waving. She ran towards me looking like an excited child. I moved up to her, but with less vigour and she drew closer, her face fell back to neutrality.

A tinge of professionalism came from her, "I guess I'm more happy to see you than you are to be here."

"Hello, you," I smiled sheepishly and leaned in to kiss her on the lips.

Ana recoiled. She looked me in the eyes, a look more of dismay than one of disgust.

"What is it?" she asked.

"Nothing, it's nice to see you. Sorry again for disappearing like that yesterday."

Ana looked down as my right arm juddered with the bag I was holding.

"What's this, you come bearing gifts? Your apology was more than enough," she said.

"It's pie from Eastmoor's finest, we can have it for

dessert."

"Leo," she sighed, as if she thought I was bribing her. "I hope you realise I've given you the same access to the Citizen Science project that anyone inside Philomena would have been given. I'd say you've had a tiny bit more. I assume you come armed with a request for further access to my father's files?"

"Actually, I just want to talk...."

I followed her back to the house. This time we entered directly from the garage via a door that led us into the living room and onto a landing. Brown speckled carpets hid any dirt and off-white walls tried to brighten the mood. The dinner table was already set, glowing under a large tealight candle. She invited me to sit, and I did so hesitantly. I was about to ask for her father but as Ana disappeared into the kitchen, her olfactory bouquet was replaced by the delicious smell of stamppot.

When she returned, she mistook the look on my face for puzzlement. "It's stamppot," she offered. "A Leidenturian specialty, fortified with vegetables that I specially chose for their aphrodisiacal qualities. Though I'm not so sure you and I are on the same page tonight." I felt her eyes trying to pierce my mind.

"Anyway, let me go fetch the meat."

I couldn't tell if Ana accepted my mood or was trying to change it. I sipped the red wine she left beside the dish and closed my eyes for a brief moment. In that tiny window of time, I noted her footsteps disappearing in the hallway, which bore the usual signature of her gait. However, it sounded quite different on the return journey, as if she had doubled in mass. There was a marching quality to it, pronounced by the driving thud of weighty boots. They were also larger gaps between the sound of each stride, and they were getting closer much faster. I instinctively opened my eyes. Shadows flickered on the wall as the candle flame jumped actively around the wick, like two fighters in a ring. The wick desperate to get the flame off him, the flame refusing to let go. Then the air thickened. The footsteps got louder until they stopped, raising the hairs on the back of my neck. A slim wedge of time, expanded by a swelling anticipation, brought a rapid lull. Then I heard the chesty voice of a man, the man I was predestined to meet, the man who took up all the space in my head like a bull elephant in a paddle pool.

"You've been looking for me, I understand."

I turned in my chair to meet the eyes of the

imposing figure looking down at me. Excitement, dread, curiosity, anxiety, anger, awe—they all fizzed under my skin at once.

"I'm Dr Raymond Strachan, the chancellor of Philomena. Ana said you might join us for dinner and that you would have questions," he slowed, "well, here I am."

Strachan moved past me and took his seat at the head of the table in the corner. My gaze was fixed upon him like a predator to its prey.

"C-it-izen… Science, Mr Strachan," I spluttered. I cleared my throat and tried again, "I wanted to discuss the program, yes."

Strachan sat back and smiled. "Eat, Leo," he said, gesturing to the dish of stamppot on the table. "There is plenty of time to discuss all these things."

He had the commanding manner of a king leading discussion in his court. Perched on his throne, he began to pour himself a glass of wine from the table. "Oh, and please, call me Ray," he said, as if trying to relax me. I felt his baritone ripple through my chair.

"Ray…" I began in earnest, remembering that Ana said he was big on dreams. "I understand that your interest in science isn't limited to physics…" I was cut off when Ana walked between us to place the meat dish down.

"Dinner is served," she said and joined us at the table.

"Uhm," I cleared my throat again, "we're just getting started." I looked at her disapprovingly.

"Okay…" she said with a stern, confused tone. She looked at me, over to her father and back at me again. "Okay," she exhaled, as if resetting the mood. "Let's start at the beginning, shall we?"

Ana started to talk about the origins of Philomena and its founders. She mentioned its large endowment fund, which "never gets touched, by the way," because of the fees, grants, and donations they continue to receive every year from the alumni. I could not pay much attention to the details of what she was saying because I was so focussed on Strachan. She spoke about their international funding too, which had its own category, for accounting purposes, and which came from the corporations in nations where their research was being conducted.

"Like Divitia. And the RMC." I blurted dryly, still locked on to her father and he to me. In ordinary circumstances I would have been impressed by the transparency of her disclosure. But I was blinkered.

She looked at me and Strachan again with incredulity. I thought that either the tension was becoming too much for her, or she despised the 'macho-nonsense,' as Sasha would say. Ana stood up, sending her chair shooting backwards. "Excuse me while I go prepare dessert for later," she said, before storming off. Strachan seemed glad. I think we both were.

"Leo, please continue. You were saying something…about…what was it?"

I got the feeling he was toying with me and my patience was wearing thin. "What is your game here?" I asked pointedly.

"No game, just research," he shot back.

"And Killaby? What's happening up there?"

Then nothing. A period of silence. Strachan choked on his words. His Adam's apple danced about his neck as he fought the tide rising within him. I imagined him stretching across the table and strangling me, effortlessly, with his bulbous hands. Judging by Ana's well-timed departure, I guessed that sudden eruptions were common with Strachan. He was trying to restrain himself; I noticed his voice change, purposely deeper in his chest and how he controlled the rhythm of his breathing.

Strachan put down his glass and rested his palms face-down on the table. "What's happening up there like what?"

"Give it a fucking rest!" My exasperation grew. "It's not just John Bishop and the like, it's my dreams…" I broke off and took a deep breath, hiding my hands beneath the table.

"I realise answers won't be forthcoming speaking to you like this. I will have to find other means."

"Are you threatening me, boy? Do yourself a favour and stay away from Killaby."

"Boy? Who are you calling boy?" I shouted. "Then it only takes a boy to know you're up to no good. And a boy to stop you."

I looked across the table at him, my eyes now shooting flaming arrows into his soul. I watched him as his palms turn to fists and his forehead crimpled under the weight of my impertinence. I had a vision of breaking my empty plate and slashing him with it. My hands tightened around the cutlery. He smiled an imperious smile, as if he knew exactly what I was thinking but was keen to prove he was undisturbed by it.

"Ahh!" Ana yelped over thrashing and smashing sounds.

"Ana? What's happened? I'm coming," I shouted out.

As she whimpered in the kitchen I stood from my chair and edged backwards cautiously, looking into Strachan's soulless eyes as I did so.

"Alright," I said, feeling my way behind me, "if you don't want to give me anything, like I said I'll find out the truth another way. Now I can see quite clearly, there is a smokescreen after all."

Strachan was breathing out like a steam engine, which was appropriate for his image. He looked very analogue, a pencil-and-paper man who would prefer a boat over a trans-Tifius supersonic jet, never mind using a mobile phone. He was old-fashioned; that did not mean I could agree with him, but it made me fear him less. I marked him then as two alphas marked each other to claim dominance over territory. My body held firm, ready to fight or run, whatever was needed. Strachan rose slowly, the spotlight above making his pale skin glow bright. He was much paler than Ana, apart from the reddish hue on the top of his bald head for which he could thank the Divitian sun.

Still holding fists, he put his knuckles on the table and leaned on to them, moving his face towards me as if to speak. He raised one arm and pointed at me angrily, poking the air between us. I continued to inch back towards Ana. His body created a large shadow on the table and what little light he did not block out directly, his dark clothing absorbed. He was like a thick, black cloud floating in on a sunny day, casting darkness everywhere.

I held my palms open behind me so I could feel when I reached the wall to the entrance of the hallway.

Ray was unhinged. "If you think I'm going to let some little upstart like you ruin my life's work then you've got another think coming," he snarled. Then to my surprise he broke into a kind of sermon. "You know what's wrong with the world Leo, what's wrong with this pitiful world? I'll tell you. People in this world will never understand. They need to be saved, Leo, all of them. They need to be saved from themselves. And from where I sit, I am the one who holds the key. My vision is an age-old vision. Yet no one has been able to find what we have found. Ana's mother, my dear wife…." Strachan tailed off sadly then restarted with menace, "…my wife Clara and I wanted to change the world. Now, I have only one mission. So, I say this to you very clearly," Strachan brought his speech to a crawl, "do not get in my way."

It was a beastlike outburst with so much power in his spiel. Each syllable of his exhortation carried its own emotional sting, like he was attacking me from inside. With my back to the wall then, I turned at once and ran to Ana in the kitchen.

In the kitchen—I was drained by Strachan's sermon—I found Ana standing by the sink cooling her hand under the running tap.

"I'm okay," she said disappointedly, looking down at the broken dish and pie strewn across the floor.

"Don't worry, I'll clean this up," I said, still gripped by talons of emotion. "And then, if you don't mind, I think I'd better go."

Ana could not bring herself to look at me while I swept the floor. I figured she was upset with her dad too, but it was pointless asking. We did our own thing in the kitchen, each without an utterance. I do not recall calling for a taxi, but it was sometime between checking on Ana and arriving back at the deserted table.

Strachan had left, I assumed back to his lair

underground where he could resume his true form. It was irrelevant anyway; I was simply relieved that he was gone. On the table lay the untouched dish of stamppot and a half-empty bottle of wine. Together they depicted the aftermath of an unsuccessful dinner. Soon my breath returned to a steadier pace. I was more perceptive of Ana's mood, her pain from the burn, and her annoyance at us both.

"Men." She nodded, looking at me with her chagrined eyes. I hoped she would lay some blame at Strachan's door too, but it was her father after all, so I bit my tongue rather than annoy her further.

On the taxi ride home, I gazed out of the back-seat window beyond the droplets streaking down the glass. I appreciated the driver keeping his thoughts to himself. The smell of the damp, floral air mixed with the rotting fruits of the Westmoor garden orchards squeezed through the crack in my window. Out in the night air, the last vestiges of the Friday night crowds walked by ghost-like streaks of lingering light which turned everything outside into gloom. Again, I sunk into a vat of memories that were swiping in and out of sight, alternating between images stored in my brain and the dark foliage that lined the streets outside. The steady hum of the car began to sooth me. Then my phone rang.

"Kev?" I answered.

I heard nothing but breathing. "Leo, it's me," he whispered in between pants and sniffles.

"Everything okay, Kev? What is it?"

"Our brother's gone Leo," the whimpering continued. "He's gone." There was more sobbing and sniffling before Kevin got a hold of himself, just for long enough to say those scarring words...

"...Jamal is dead."

CHAPTER 14

Making landfall, I looked down at the white water of the foaming ocean dissipating with the crashing waves, watching the sea and terrain in their eternal dance of fluidity and resistance. The rolling brown hills and subtle green landscape went quietly below, tucked under the whistling rush of wind. That sense of freedom, unencumbered by the limitations of the physical world, initially made this place one in which I would have preferred to reside, until I descended from the sky and landed softly in the garden of number 36 Mount Providence. The front door of the bungalow opened as my feet touch the tiled foot path.

"You're right on time," Jamal's mother said, holding a steaming sponge cake with mittens, "this just came out of the oven." She was smiling. No, she was jubilant. "Come in," she continued, "Jamal is on his way..."

I woke up with a knotted stomach and eyes full of

tears. I cut the dream short. I do not know how I did it. This dream was a Cerise dream. Cerise meaning—according to my system of dream classification—it was overwhelming. Until then, all the Cerise dreams I have ever had had a shattering effect that threw me violently out of sleep. This time I pulled the emergency cord myself, from within the dream, extending a sort of conscious control over it, like a fighter pilot ejecting from high-speed flight. I exited without so much as a glance backwards.

The feeling in the dream, that rising sickness, a churning in the gut and a flame climbing up the trachea—I suppressed it with a forceful swallowing action. Not puking on myself was a false comfort and I knew it. Like pouring a glass of water on a burning pan of oil. When I woke to full alertness, the memory connected with the dream was packed away in a tiny little box, deep beneath the floorboards of the basement in my mind.

It took a little more time to move, but I accepted I was back in Divitia, in my own bed—for real. The aliveness that I had when I was with Ana leaked away, along with any feelings of, well, anything. I returned to that desolate place of numbness, deafness, and tastelessness, a triangulation matched by no other time in history except, perhaps, after Sasha deserted me.

My phone buzzed non-stop on my bedside table. Messages came for hours, some from Ana, a few from old school friends and everyone I did not want to hear from. Nothing from Sasha though. A call from her would have been the soothing ointment to my weeping wounds. I thought of her more than I cared to admit to myself.

The investigation into Jamal's death was short. Cause of death: blunt force trauma.

"I was told they got the truck driver," said Den by text, not seeing the fruitlessness of the arrest. Perhaps it gave him comfort.

"There is some justice at least," Xavier replied.

"It won't bring him back, will it?" Kevin texted, summing up my thoughts. I felt that his anger was laced with the soft tone of regret.

"Just got a message from Uncle Curtis, the funeral is next Friday," Dennis typed.

I contributed nothing to the group chat. They acknowledged Dennis as we each fell back onto our own mechanisms of coping. I would have been J's dad's point of contact, if his messages had not been lost in the heap of condolences. My mind had already moved itself to a place to which it was well acclimatised. Have you ever seen a new fish added to an established aquarium? It darts around in hyper-activity looking for places to hide, hoping to settle in the safe crevices of aqua rock or in the camouflage of an underwater plant. My mind did just that and came to settle happily at the bottom of a large bottle of whiskey, rum—whatever I could get my hands on. If I became thirsty, I quenched my thirst with lager.

Opportunities come from the strangest places, I thought in one of my drunken states of lassitude and rejoiced in the deliverance that mindlessness afforded. Day by day went by like that. Until the dreaded day of the funeral itself.

CHAPTER 15

On the morning of J's funeral, we were heading to meet with family and friends at Uncle Curtis' place in advance of the procession to Eastmoor Palms Crematorium. Kevin's car was a rolling container of cigarette smoke, wet pinecones, and old citrus. Sometimes it carried people too, and was regretfully the vehicle most suited to a funeral procession. A few early comments from Xavier and Dennis told me that they were well aware of Kevin's new smoking habit: another one of a catalogue of things I missed over the previous months. Without J around, I was truly the orphan of the gang. Heading in a south-westerly direction, closer to the border with Westmoor but more toward the valley, 'the Crem' was the prettiest place that no one wanted to be. We were destined for one of the most ornate buildings in Divitia outside of the presidential palace. Not a squeak further came from any of us on the short ride across town. Not the tooting of horns or arguments on the street corners, the cawing of crows or barking of dogs, not even the rattle of the car's suspension across the potholes disturbed the peace inside. It was not a peace-of-the-soul kind of peace; the one that brings a contented heart and still mind, but an auditory peace; the type that brings brow-bending apprehension, sweaty anxiety, and palpitating visions. Imagining J's beaten body in the casket was sufficient to have this effect. Eastmoor itself appeared dressed for occasion too. The buildings, trees, streets, and passers-by were all colourless. The mood in the car seemed to spill out and douse the whole town grey. Even the sky.

Xavier was first to break the quiet. "I wonder what J would say if he could see us like this."

"He'd probably ask why we're all wearing black, like if someone died."

Dennis looked around at each of us. Perhaps a little jiggle in the body even a cough, would have been close enough to a laugh for Den, but he might just as well have been looking off the edge of a cliff, in the middle of the night, at the bottom of the ocean.

"Your jokes are not only untimely, Den, but they're shit," Xavier replied.

"Well," said Den, "He'd definitely ask Leo if he mistook the whiskey bottle for cologne."

My eyelids were heavy. I did not even hear the comment until Kevin repeated it in my defense. He said something to Dennis about allowing people to deal with things in their own way.

"Ignore him, Leo, some people are born that way," he said.

"Born with insolence?" Xavier added.

I looked out the window. I knew Dennis had no ill intent, just ill timing. He was trying to lift the mood and even I understood that at a basic level.

Kevin pulled up in front of Uncle Curtis' house. He was already outside, surrounded by a large group of well-wishers reaching for him. I looked across at Kevin sat in the driver's seat and out of his window, seeing Uncle Curtis swimming in a sea of black, with arm after arm, like octopuses stretching out from the dark pool of grief and wrapping their tentacles around him. I felt for him, standing there, having to bear this all on his own as I stared on from the front passenger seat. Kevin could not look, his face forwards, staring into space. I watched a single tear pop out his quivering eye and roll down his cheek. Kevin scarcely showed emotion, even hearing him whimpering on the phone the week before when telling me about Jamal's death was painful. To make it even worse for him, he was already sore from his aunt's death just 10 months before and that was the only time I knew Kevin to cry. She was really his mother because she raised him for a large proportion of his life, taking care of him when his birth mother moved to Ferrumterre to help with the healing on that continent after the genocide. When his aunt succumbed to a short, painful struggle with cancer, Kev's tears ran like a broken tap. That evening we went drinking, graduating from pale ales, to lagers, to whiskey liqueurs and then gin. It started with patient sips of lubrication. First, he became reminiscent, then angry, then polemical, then whiney, then blissful, and then stomach-churning drunk. I listened for a while, then held him as he cried and pressed his forehead into my shoulder, sobbing into my lapel until it dangled, sodden, under the weight of his anguish.

I sat in his car then, watching this all unfold; Uncle Curtis, Kevin, family, and friends assembling outside, the grey nothingness of it all contaminated everything my eyes met.

Dennis and Xavier hugged Uncle Curtis. The point

at which they left the car, slammed the doors shut and crossed the street in front of us did not so much as scratch the veil of my gaze.

"We should go," Kevin suggested, noting our absence from the fold as being, "unbecoming."

I obeyed without protest. We joined the pool around him where more hugs and condolences were shared out. All I thought for Uncle Curtis was that he must have been tired and, if he were not feeling it yet, that it would be imminent. A strengthening breeze caused his Dashiki to flap like a flag in the wind, a wind that brought dark clouds—and the hearse with Jamal's body.

The street fell silent in a wave, from the sweet shop on the corner at the top of the incline, down to the barber shop in the middle, to us, and then up to the children's park on the opposite end. The road dipped in a U shape, but shallower; it was between that and gentler curves of a tablespoon. The hearse stopped, let the funeral director out, and then crawled behind his theatrical march to the house, giving neighbours the chance to pay their respects. Uncle Curtis's flapping garments disguised his low snivels to most, but not me; I was attuned to the hallmarks of pain. When the hearse stopped in front of the house, we dipped our heads in respect and made a quick turn for our cars and to begin the procession to the Crem.

The ride there passed without notice as the four of us sat back into our previous spaces of dread. Jamal's hulking black hearse arrived at the Crem entrance, down the palm-lined driveway and to the valley that stretched miles into the foot of Killaby. I fiddled my fingers in my breast pocket for my eulogy notes, grabbing the rum miniature at the same time. Thankfully, Dennis kept his mouth shut.

The rum burned my insides though it was tasteless. It fulfilled its role however, to soften the exit from the car behind J's casket and the following of it into the waiting crowd. Inside the crematorium, every detail of the funeral service started according to J father's wishes. The priest did his bit quickly, some cried, others sat stony faced. I must have looked stony faced too, perhaps a little more relaxed than the others, who did not benefit from the effects of 60% proof Divitian white rum. Cries and coughs echoed around the grand room, snotty breathing rumbled amidst the mannequin-like folks, and then there was Jamal's aunty. She was over to the far right side of the mourners, breaking down into sudden fits of hysterics. She had only just arrived from Makhzwane that morning, so I figured her jet lag contributed to her outburst. Her body flung itself to the tiles and contorted into shapes that made her spine look like rubber. There was the arching of her back off the floor, the bending of her neck so her ear touched her shoulder, and the collapsing of her wrists so that her hands twisted inward and stayed there. She was beyond the comfort of those around her. It was not so much her limbs, appearing to contain a foreign entity that was desperate to escape, but it was the way her torso got bounced around from the inside that suggested possession. I sought out Uncle's Curtis' face; it was empty, like a canvas waiting to be painted. I imagined that losing Jamal's mother; his one true love, and then his only son, would make this display of sorrow humorous to him. Then I kicked myself for thinking such thoughts, disappointed with them for holding no morsels of compassion. Then it was my time to read the eulogy.

I walked up a couple of steps to the left of the open casket without casting a single glance at J. A lectern overlooked him where I placed my notes. From that perch I could not see his body and I was grateful for it.

I saw a sea of faces with their eyes dancing between me and Jamal below. Unfolding the paper from my pocket, I could hardly raise my chin from my chest looking as if I were peering outwards over invisible spectacles. With a low, dry voice, I started.

"I'm-I'm going, I'm going to keep this very short because Jamal hated long boring speeches, especially my long boring speeches," I said, hoping to open with a joke. It was clear that humour was also about the delivery and, reaction I got said that I was incapable of meeting that standard. "No one goes through life expecting to die even though we know death is inevitable. Even with the certainty of death, it is decoupled from our everyday life so that we continue to live as if it would never meet us at the end of the road. And while we know somewhere in the back of our minds that it will come for us, and make no mistake it will come, unfortunately, it came way too early for my dear friend Jamal Field. It was only a couple of weeks ago that J came to me at my home to pull me up and out of my languor. He was the only one who could get through my wall of resistance and yank me from one of the darkest, holes I have ever known but…"

A lump forming in my throat started to choke me

when I conjured images of J standing outside my room under Grandfather, "...but I never thanked him for it. I never thanked him for anything he did for me. And now he's gone there will be no more daily check-ups at my door, no one looking out for me, no persistent calls when I go missing, no wisecracks or smart remarks, with J gone there will be no more of the same," I raised my chin from my chest and looked into the crowd, "who will get me out of the hole that I'm in now?"

I know it sounded selfish. My best friend died in a tragedy and all I could think of was myself. If my voice was bountiful with life rather than the dry, flaking husk of sentiment, then perhaps the congregation might have appreciated the meaning behind it. Since I prepared all those remarks it appeared that I was adamant to finish in spite of its limpness. In fact, I was swallowed by the words on the page, and oblivious to the cues from Dennis and the gang that I should consider wrapping up. So, I went on reading and talking about our past and that we were like brothers. Convention dictated that I should 'share a personal story of the deceased,' so I did that. I told them about infants' school when our friend Vijay shat himself. Poor Vij, none of the school kids wanted to be near him. Obviously, I wanted to run away too, but J kept me there. He did not have to say anything because it was the way he looked at me, then at Vijay sorrily, and back at me again. If his 5-year-old eyes could speak they would just say love. J was the only one who cared enough not to scorn Vijay but instead offered help. My monotonic discourse continued.

"How many kids do you know with the presence of mind and strength of character to show such kindness when the herd was doing the opposite? It was a gesture befitting the man we came to know and love deeply and a quality he kept to the end."

I went on a bit about secondary school too and shared a couple more stories that reflected J's character in a Jesus-like glow. It was not that it was not true, but more that I did not do the eulogy justice. Like the soft meowing of a lion, or a musician who did not want to play; the sound came out, but the heart was lacking.

I finished the eulogy in much the same manner, folded the paper and put it back into my pocket. On the way back to my perch at the edge of the seating area there was a rumbling in my stomach—like butterflies, but bat-sized—when the priest passed me on the stairs and nodded as if to say, 'I understand.' I looked down fast, settling my chin on its grooved seat in my chest to avoid welcoming such an intrusion and then, just as swiftly as my eyes went down, they were over-powered by the lure of Jamal's corpse. Lure is the right word. Not that it was attractive at all but it was that I fought with the desire to look at it on the first trip up to the lectern in much the same way that one struggles to look away from the bodies trapped in a high-speed wreck. I did not recognise it. Whether it was the embalming that swelled him, the makeup covering his injuries or the stitching in his skull from the autopsy, it was too late to erase. The churning in my stomach grew into a bubbling stew, the lump in my throat swelled to the size of a grapefruit and when the pressure became too much bear, it vented upwards to my face, heating it from the friction of the racing blood flow and overwhelming my eyes to bursting point. I moved hurriedly to the male facilities toward the back and side of the gathering via a corridor hidden behind a decorative brick wall. The faster I walked was the faster my tears seemed to flow. A quick look back relieved any worry that my emotions might be seen.

Amid this eruption, the burning call of my mother coming in caught my attention even though when she came in fully, she said nothing. It was like she was in my head, but only watching. I entered the bathroom and doused my face with furious pats of cold water, since the offish chill of the Divitian summer breeze was not cool enough to dampen the flare-up. Already the burning from mum was subsiding but there was another feeling coming up, or something like a feeling, disconnected from my physical senses yet drawing my attention to a presence. Interesting it was for me to have felt the arrival of my mother, but not to have heard her. Then, while patting my face and looking in the mirror, to have seen her was more alarming.

"Hello my son..."

The image in the mirror could not be denied. Behind my right shoulder her unmistakable, flawless brown skin shimmered in the bathroom light. I doused my face again then squinted into the glass, "Mum?" My voice discovered a new, higher octave. When mother walked over to me, the calm reassurance of her palm on my back was proof enough that this was not a dream.

"I had to come," she said, sensing my speeding heart. She was perceptive enough to see my mind straining to catch up to the reality.

"You are not dreaming, darling," she said, without moving her lips.

The disbelief was still there but my pulse shifted downwards from the up-tempo rhythms of funky house to something more sedentary. Leaning forward with both of my hands gripping the sides of the sink I continued to stare, looking for a glitch or flicker, and weary that mother might vanish as quickly as she appeared.

"I didn't see you in the crowd. When did you get in? How long have you been here? Did you see my eulogy?" I stood still holding on, squeezing the blood out of my fingertips until they turned blue.

"I just arrived, Leo. Come give your mother a hug," she gestured, rotating her hands around her wrists towards her and speaking out in the open for the first time. Her arms outstretched toward me with the same grace of an albatross. I faced mother for the first time in years, I understood why my father called her Daisy. Not only did she look young, she held a gentle luminosity, like the filament of bulb-less light. When I turned and walked into her open arms, her small body enveloped in full. I sobbed as one would expect a young child to cry in their mother's arms but with less dramatics.

"I'm sorry to hear about Jamal, may God rest his soul. I pray for him and his family and I take solace in the knowledge that he has returned from whence he came." Mother said with a surety, even if solemnly and sometimes in ways I didn't understand. "I came forth from the Father and have come to the world and so I must leave the world, and go on unto the Father. Jamal is fine, Leo. And soon you will be too…" she paused, raised her cheek from the top of my head and looked directly into my soul, "…but only if that is what you want, Leo. Now stand up," she said, putting her arms beneath my armpits as if to lift me, "and dust of your knees." I stood again and looked down at my mother and she back up at me. "So, what do you want?" she asked. "A lot has happened, I understand that. But you are here now. You can, if you want to, go back to your house and lie in your bed of sorrow. You can drink your way back down to that abysmal place you were in and repeat the cycle—over and over again—, or you can continue moving forward. You can get those answers you seek. You said you wanted answers, didn't you?

"Yes."

You seemed to have found purpose in the Citizen

Science program, didn't you?"

"Yes."

"You said you wanted to see what lies behind the surface, didn't you?"

"Yes." I said again, turning back to face the mirror.

"I believe in you, Leo. You have the will inside you. You have the conviction inside you. Just tap into it. Find that power within you to keep moving forward." My mother went quiet while I digested her words. Her break seemed timed to change the direction of thought, from her-to-me, to me-to-her. "What do you really want to do from this point?" she said, reverting to tele-speak.

"About Citizen Science?" I said aloud, peering into the darkness of the drain hole. "Well, I just want…the truth."

"Then that is what you should seek."

A slight breeze brushed my cheek accompanied by a lingering air of rose oil blowing over, somewhat delayed, like the slow roll thunder after the flash of light. There was no hug or formal goodbye, or even the collapsing sound of a vanishing poof. The only evidence I had that mother was there was slowly floating out the bathroom window and into the Divitian sky.

CHAPTER 16

"I don't know what's going with you or why you're treating me this way but please, call me, I need to speak with you as soon as possible. There's been a break-in and they've totally ransacked the basement library. I've done a thorough stocktake and most of the stuff can be recovered but they took my father's dagboek, Leo. Please, when you get this message call me back. What's worse, is I've never even been allowed to see what he kept in that diary and Daddy knew they would try to take it. He knew, Leo, he just knew! Call me."

Ana's many voice messages were angry. Or maybe she was concerned—it was hard to tell through a jumble of shrieks and breathy words, tamed by light sprinkling of hopeful calm. That last panicky message fanned the flames of my determination though because somewhere out there, any one of the millions of cars creating the steady hum of the Divitian rush hour could have been transporting the Chancellor's journal. That possibility, along with my urge to refocus on Philomena mixed in my veins with a fresh dose of caffeine. When I returned Ana's call she answered instantly.

"Thank God. I need to see you; how soon can we meet?"

"As soon as you can get here," I replied.

"Okay, but my father…" she broke off, "…not on the phone. I'll tell you when I get there."

Within an hour, Ana was stepping over empty bottles and cans to get into my kitchen. There were no pleasantries, though I was duty-bound to explain that "my best friend died and, well, you know, all the things that come with that."

"I'm so, so sorry, Leo," she said as she hugged me. "I had no idea and here I am making this all about me."

The weight of Ana's arms around my neck kept me grounded for a time. Her eyes explored all the empty drinks containers that littered the floor. She looked at me again—one eyebrow almost touching her hairline, the other depressed into a quizzical wrinkle.

"What? I'm good," I said. "I'm back in the saddle now and more ready than ever to get to get back to work. Anyway, what's the whole deal with your father's book?"

The way Ana slid her hands from around my neck, down my shoulders and gripped my wrists impressed upon me the severity of her concern.

"That dagboek meant the world to him. I swore to him I would keep it safe."

"Ana, help me to help you," I stressed. "What am I missing here? Why would anyone break into a house in Westmoor, and only take a private journal?"

"Okay, okay," she said with a sigh as she stepped back and perched on the kitchen table. "It's to do with a classified part of his research, but that's about the extent of my knowledge on it. My father always kept me away from that side of things even though I am one of the teaching staff and his damn daughter. Strange right?"

"To protect you, maybe?"

"It's possible. He also spoke of a group he called the HOIB. I don't know who they are or anything of his relationship to them, but he made me promise him one thing -never let anyone know about the dagboek. He's been a pretty paranoid man his whole life."

"So why are you so involved in finding the book now? I mean, why don't you let your father clean this mess up himself?"

"What? What do you mean?! Leo…" Ana's phone rang and cut her. The sorry soul who called her from the university felt the full force of her exasperation. Then the phone had its turn to feel it, which she sent skating across the kitchen counter until it was stopped dead by the tiled wall on the far end.

Everyone has a breaking point and I knew that any further prodding would have cost much more than the worth of any insights Ana could give. Plus, there must have been only one place the chancellor could have been at a time like that. I sensed an opportunity.

I was keen not to indulge Ana in any further conversation on this—not just because I wanted to protect her, or because I feared she might leak my plans to her father—but it was a form of compartmentalisation that I felt was needed if she and I were to have any possibility of a future together.

"I understand," I said. "You know I'm here for you but honestly, I need to take some time out, especially after the funeral and everything. I just need a little bit of time to pull myself together."

"Okay, Leo," she said as she lowered her head, "I can't say I'm happy about that but I understand. Just swear to me that you will never breathe a word of this conversation again—not even to me."

I nodded with respect and started to the bedroom for my holdall.

"Going somewhere?" she asked.

"I'm only heading to the monastery for a few days. It feels like a good time to switch off and recharge."

"The one on Killaby? Let me take you."

I packed up and took a final glance at my bedroom. If Grandfather could have spoken through the window, he would have imparted some words of impassive wisdom, perhaps something about appreciating the fruits available closer to home, and he probably would have spoken in Jamal's voice. He allowed some light through his leaves and into the room, shining narrow beams onto Sasha's crumpled letter and on the family photo next to it. I snapped my focus back to the direction of travel—Killaby.

CHAPTER 17

Even after many years of working and living in Divitia, Ana still was not used to driving on the other side of the road and the narrower they got, the less confidence I had in her.

"Not far now," she said, pointing to the road sign. "See? Killaby Monastic College, 3 miles."

"However long it takes."

Ana tried to make conversation without talking about her father, but that was a feat only accomplished thespians could do. Our minds were each fixed on their own objects of obsession and, while hers was obscured by the sediment of doubt, my intentions lay pellucidly in the heart of Killaby. I thought about Strachan, his diary, and what made him tick.

"Ana, would you mind if I asked about your mother?" I asked.

"Strange thing to be on your mind after everything you've just been through. Why?"

"I guess you just haven't spoken much about her."

"There is a lot you are yet to learn about me, Leo, but sure, I can tell you. My mother was called Clara. She was a scientist like dad. She worked closely with dad on research, but things didn't work out."

"Between them? Or do you mean the work didn't work out?"

"Yeah, the latter, I guess."

"What were they researching?"

"Not a million miles away from what we're doing right now—research into natural phenomena."

"Well, that's pretty broad. A family doctor could claim to be looking into natural phenomena."

"I only have my father's word on this, because it was meant to be secret but they were leading an experiment over a hundred storeys beneath the Alps of Ventura back in Leidenturia. Something obviously went wrong down there because daddy came back, mum didn't."

"Do you know what went wrong?"

"Something to do with the experiment." She said.

I waited for further explanation. Nothing arrived.

"Into natural phenomena?" I asked again.

"Yes, Leo!"

I did not need to say more, thanks to the crushing sounds of stones under the tyres breaking me away from the questioning and sparing me her frustration. The road to the monastery was long and loud. Ana looked fascinated to see the tip of Killaby from such an acute angle, made more imposing by the tilt of the sun, which had passed overhead and started to warm the leeward side of the mountain. Some of the stones ricocheted like mini explosions under the tyre pressure, livening up our arrival through the thickening woodland.

At the reception car park, Ana leant over and hugged me. "See you soon?"

Her embrace took the chill off her words and, since her mask had fallen, it was just as difficult for me not to see the true Ana, as it was for her to hide it. I leant into her and kissed her with a flat sense of duty, "See you on the other side."

Getting out of her car was like walking off the edge of the Earth. It must have been how my parents felt as colonial subjects, waving goodbye to all that they knew from the decks of foreign ships sailing away to new lands. I sensed Ana staring into my back as I walked over to reception, distracting me from the monastery grounds with guest lodges that lay dotted around the site. Then a flash of Strachan's face—growling like rabid dog—blinded me to the step at the door in front.

"Mind your step!" shouted the monk at reception. "And welcome to the Killaby Monastic College. On a self-retreat?"

"Something like that," I muttered. "I'd also like to get into the forest, maybe."

"Ah yes, there has been so much activity up there lately," he said. "I'm new here, but others here say they don't remember a time when there has been such interest in the mountain."

"Oh really? Do you know where they are going?"

"Yeah, come over here—" he said, walking out from behind his desk. He walked beside me to the door and pointed up the hill. "Just up there, you see? Where those large rocks are, sort of middle-ish, toward the top third?"

"Uh huh."

"Right up there."

He gave me the keys to a cabin.

"Thanks for your help," I said.

"Hey, if you do go up there, be very careful."

My south-facing lodge was a five minute walk through the woods behind the main monastery building.

I walked on, looking up at the mountain and organising my thoughts, like ordering a deck of cards in which Strachan was the ace.

At the cabin, I dropped my bag beside an old wooden chair and a dark matching table. Sunlight filled the lodge with its twinkling shapes, but the room was bare, designed minimally, to leave one alone with their thoughts and feelings. The sweetness of the truth was more compelling; it melted on my tongue took over my body, moving it toward the door, toward satiation. Each step driven by something other than my conscious thought. The first few steps took me out of the room and into the waiting wood. The footpath was obvious at first, fusing into one continuous slab from several different routes that were snaking outwards from the cabins. My thoughts came and went of their own accord. Those of Strachan stayed as I gazed downwards, watching the path evolve beneath my boots from the smooth, marked paving of the monastery grounds to a narrow line in the soil, defined only by constant traipsing. Brickwork made way for black earth, decorated with small stones and the odd blade of wild grass, all squashed into a flat mixture and baked firm.

Hours went by. I stopped to sip on some water from my backpack. The wood became forest, and the forest became jungle. To my left, a large, rounded rock offered a good perch for me to sit and think. If I could have seen myself, I would have seen a man armed with no plan but a broad, loosely articulated wish to get to the truth, guided by generous portions of guile, strong instinct and a side helping of fortitude. I did not know to what degree those images were delusional.

A sharp breeze tickled the branches above; their denseness gave the impression of night. Still, outside retained more light than the black hole eating its way through me. I pressed my lips together until they hurt, hoping to contain the pressure building in the back of my throat. *Mystery within mystery*, I thought. I felt it strange how anticipation, anger, anguish, elation all registered in me the same way; they ticked away in my neck like a grenade waiting to explode. I just did not know what kind of blast to expect. It could have been anywhere between exultant fireworks in the night sky and the dismally destructive mushroom cloud of a nuclear explosion. A transitory memory of Sasha and the boys reared its head and its fists and pounded my heart, followed by stomach-churning images of Dante and Eli, with Strachan's face on both of their heads. And they sounded like Jamal. *Focus on the truth, Leo, on Strachan!* I counselled myself.

Out of the bamboo bush behind me, a thin green snake slithered, if only to warn me and sharpen my alertness to a sound approaching in the distance. Leaves were being squashed beneath footsteps and grew louder. Looking around and hoping to spot the source of the sound proved futile, since its movements were in opposite sync with me; when I moved, it stopped, when I stopped, it moved. This game of cat and mouse—in which I was the mouse—was not a fun game at all.

Crouching was the better choice then, even if jagged rocks opened my knees to the air and thorny vines perforated my palms. Nothing could be worse than dying before I got my answers, only to end up as a tormented soul in heaven—if that was where I was destined. I crawled for some distance backwards, hugging the large rock where I was previously sat and wedged myself behind it. I craved the feeling of safety, but it was impossible to summon.

Divitia was famed for its predators—large wild cats, over-sized constrictors, and the indigenous Fresden

Dragon. If it were indeed my time to die, and I had to go by one of those creatures, the Fresden would be my last choice. The grizzly-sized reptile, like a Comodo Dragon—with a face, less gecko and more crocodile—had been blamed for several disappearances around the country. That was hard to accept since I knew no Divitians who had ever seen a Fresden. Either way, its legend struck the same chord of terror.

Levelheadedness eluded me, so running for it seemed as good a choice as any. Around 200 metres ahead lay a large clearing of grass and shrubs before the forest started properly at a line of trees. I started sprinting so that my heels hit my butt cheeks like the crank arms of pistons, gambling that safety lay in the forest on the other side. Running was like flying. Only the whistling of wind in my ears and the flapping of my wind breaker around my waist was louder than sounds of thuds and grunts chasing me. The treeline bounced in my blurred vision with the impact of my feet on the lumpy ground. My body found reserves from somewhere, for I must have been running at least 50% faster than I had ever run before.

As the grunting got louder, that awful smell arrived, the rottenness from Ana's basement library. It got stronger with the narrowing gap between us. I was wrong to think my whole life would flash before me—the only thing I could see was the tree line ahead.

I felt a sharp, sudden pain in my back—but as though I was struck from inside. Like the tip of a knife scraping my organs before the surface wound had a chance to register. I fell forwards under a force twice my own weight, hitting the ground in front of the trees and crashing headfirst into the hard mud. That blow set off an elaborate show of firecrackers inside my skull, and then there was blackness.

CHAPTER 18

I came back from the darkness, opening my eyes, breathing in the green damp scent of earth. My mind, so artfully arranged like a deck of cards, had come undone, shook out into chaos as would a flock of birds scampering from the trees. Strachan was still in my head somewhere; it was only a matter of time before mental order resumed and I could place him back on top. Out of the disorientation came a panic that yanked me into an upright position. I searched my body for wounds and found none—I only had the memory of them. Bruised hands and knees and a stiff shoulder were the worst I could find.

Killaby forest sung a marching symphony. Without it, I might have stayed down but I dusted off what I could and continued my ascent, encouraged by the mountain's tune. *If Jamal could see me now,* I thought, embracing for a moment one of the many ponderings I had had since his death. I spared a thought for my mother as well, whose absence surprised me.

Air rolling down the mountain hissed on its surface and the invisible creatures crooned along with it. Underneath that was a low deep pulse, on the edge of the envelope of human hearing. In the corner of my eye, popped the red cheeks of fruits in a towering tree ahead. It was not an ordinary tree—it was laden with remembrances. Large, drooping cashew apples were face-tinglingly sour but that never stopped J and I from stealing them during our 'operation catcher' missions in Eastmoor growing up. I hoped that if he could see me, he would be proud that I had left the mindless stupor he rescued me from the week before he died. The rest of the cashew tree conjured up memories of Grandpa, my mother's father, whose penchant for the fruit and their seeds earned him the moniker Papa Anacardo. Papa's words came to me as I climbed to within touching distance of the clouds. "A man is strong with a good woman by his side, but he is nothing without himself." I assumed the meaning of such a statement increased in value the older you got, similar to an aged whiskey or a collector's wine.

Through a thin space between those memories and my present reality shone little glimmers of understanding. Those gaps, I learned, were my windows of emotion. I imagined my mother's voice, recounting tales of Papa as if she were in my head.

"Everybody called him Papa Anacardo. Me? I just called him Daddy," she said, with a smile that warmed her voice. "He sometimes called it 'kindle leaf', did you know that?"

Because it was used to heal people, I thought. I may have even spoken it out loud, but my mother was not really there so it did not matter. As the slopes steepened my pace slowed, my attention rotated between outside and in, as though stuck in a revolving door.

Mother's voice continued, "When I was small, I was very close to your Papa. You were named after him, if you remember. I know you only knew him as Papa. Anyway, there was a time, when I was around eight, maybe nine, when I was so sick..." Mother's voice played like a recording on repeat. I knew the story well, but I was not ready for its effect on me. It was weird. Like how you can listen to the playback of a favourite song and it makes you smile or dance, and at other times the same song folds you into tears.

Mother had an unusually strong strain of tropical fever back then, and my grandparents were sure she was going to die. To fathom losing a child of eight meagre years must have been gut-wrenching. Until that point my mother had been a bouncy little girl, effervescent with joy. Papa especially hated seeing her laid out in bed waiting for death to take her. He treated her sickness with tea from the leaves of the cashew tree, combined with some other old remedies that involved candles and cupping of the solar plexus.

My mother said, "Daddy called Mummy and my six siblings into the room. I was barely conscious, my breaths so shallow they were almost imperceptible, unless you listened very closely."

Picturing my mother as a little girl was strange for me, so to imagine her—so frail, suffering, weak, a bed-ridden child doubled over in pain, without the energy to complain, to make requests or to move to a more comfortable position—was unwelcome. A little girl so loved, and with so much promise, about to die and leave her parents in eternal agony. I started to see Papa in my mind's eye, along with my grandmother, my aunts and uncle all coming around her bed to say their goodbyes. It was a strange, horrid vision, creating a reality in my head that would essentially erase me from existence.

A cool gust blew across and a trickle of tears on my face, brought me out of the reminiscing and back onto Killaby again. Papa was dead and I missed him. My mother's own brush with death struck fear into me about losing her too, as preposterous as the idea sounds. If she had died then, there would be no me. There would have been no me and Sasha, no Dante and Eli, and there would be no investigation into Citizen Science.

My body moved by a separate engine completely, a pepper pot of feelings feeding the trembling in my knees and the quickening of my breath. I paused for another drink of water, a lot more ground needed to be covered.

The sun's angle grew sharper, its light dimmed by clouds rumbling in the distance. I was struck by the sight of a man at just the right slant so that when my eyelids wiped the water away, they showed me clearly, the unmistakable figure of Ray Strachan. It could not have been anyone else, in that location, on that day. His wide shoulders were hunched, shifting his centre of gravity so that his weight helped him forward. He was on his own, marching upwards to the same location I was destined. I watched him tentatively and followed at a distance—close enough to see him but far enough not to be heard.

My track was a rudimentary rambling route until that point. Strachan's way was different—it cut much of the distance and saved up to an hour of hiking. He was making his way through the vegetation where the path was only clear to those who knew what they were looking for. It bore no track in the mud, but when I walked it, I noticed there were some parts lightly flattened by footsteps, drawing an irregular line where no branches or vines stretched across.

As Strachan walked faster, I did too. His dark jeans and black cap made it hard to track him through the gaps in the bush. Two sharp turns in quick succession later, I lost him. I stopped at the last turn marked by a fallen tree and scanned the bushes, especially the dark crevices that dense wood afforded. Breaking branches underfoot went off like miniature explosions, followed by the slapping sound of footsteps in a shallow puddle.

"Hello again, Leo," said Strachan. His voice came from a deep, hollow place, ricocheting around the wood as if everywhere at once. "How thoughtful of you to join me all the way up here."

I turned a full rotation clockwise and back the other

way, but he hid himself well. Holding my position, the would-be chaser had become prey. Mother's voice had left me completely by then, abandoning me to the throes of my own ideas and spasms of dread. Pleased that no one could see how my confidence evaporated, I inched forward, struggling to disguise indecision in my steps. The raindrops were getting bigger, from little scratchy morsels on the face to larger shreds, falling like glass.

"Strachan!" I shouted at the top of my voice, and again, and again. "You devil! You criminal!" I was desperate to provoke him, doing whatever I could to draw him out.

"Ray," I shouted. "Getting too close, am I?"

"Too close for who?" came the answer amid an echo of pattering raindrops.

I looked around again, and again—nothing. "I'm here now, Ray. It's only a matter of time," I told him.

"Yes, it is," he agreed sardonically. "You made a grave mistake coming here, boy."

A screaming crack of thunder blared out over the town, sending sharp blades of water down from the sky, and I prepared for the coming storm.

CHAPTER 19

The trees gave little away besides sweet damp fragrance. Strachan was seen when he wanted to be seen and heard when he wanted to be heard. I had seen him more in my nightmares. There was still some way to go to the get to the clearing and I knew I was getting close, not just from the discordant feeling in my gut, but from the way the path started widening out and how the gradient flattened, also offering me a ledge of respite.

I thought I would wait him out there, seeking shelter somewhere under the trees since the heavens appeared to be in no mood to show me mercy. My mind slushed around its old route, dominated by the same people and ideas: Strachan and his intentions, Philomena and the HOIB (and obliquely the RMC), Jamal, and Dante and Eli. I got that feeling again when I thought about J. The thoughts of J were not the nostalgic thoughts of a young sage incarnated in the body of my best friend.

Rather, they were the hostile memories of a churning in my gut that came when I saw his dead body at the funeral. The memories churned and churned, spinning themselves into a new kind of pain, one that gorged on itself like a snake swallowing its own tail.

What little light remained above the mountain scarcely pierced the clouds. Underneath the clouds, a deep blue hue gave me some visibility of a small clearing. Raindrops turned back into drizzle and that brought a hush to the mountain. Behind the mating calls of croaking frogs and crickets, a curious sound came through. It would have been pleasant had the circumstances been different, had I not been jumping at every sudden twitch of the leaves. It was not blood-curdling either. It came from behind me, over a neat line of bush that hid a peculiar part of the mountain. I moved quietly toward the sound—an ensemble of voices that were not quite singing, not quite talking either—emanating from within a near-perfect circle of thick green roses. The hedge, which looked to be marking a boundary, was ineffective at hiding the unusual deep throated vibrations coming out and splitting into harmonics. They got louder as I approached, deafening against the backdrop of stillness. I felt as though I was entering a zone of beautiful accordance—like a choir singing in an oasis in the middle of a hostile desert. That melodic sound was self-evident, but nowhere before had I seen rain falling so flawlessly straight, no force acting upon it other than gravity.

In the stillness, I peered through the hedge hoping to catch sight of what, or who was inside the circle. I failed to see beyond the green Divitian roses, so densely flowered across the hedgerow. Those roses were incredibly special to the Divitian people; I was drawn to them because they reminded me of Sasha. Strachan was still on my mind. J was also there, but those roses—casting their thorns into the deep recesses of my mind and pulling Sasha right up to the top— got me thinking of a bouquet of Divitian roses that I sent to her office for our anniversary. A box of deluxe chocolates would have sufficed—I was never really a 'flower guy', even if they were the rarest—but when Sash kept accusing me of having 'too much machismo' I was desperate to prove her wrong. She called me from work that day and told me that I had "made her happier with this one gesture than all of previous years combined."

"Traditional romance may not be my forte, babe,

but I do have my moments of brilliance."

Pictures of Sash overcame me, stuck in my mind like frozen pixels on a crashed computer screen. I remembered her gregariousness and how fond my family was of her.

My attention returned to the wet bush of Killaby. Strachan's presence hung in the air like an arctic wind even if I could not see him. Had he been looking at me from the cover of darkness, he would not have been able to tell the raindrops from tears on my cheeks. I faced the hedge again and moved to my left, following its circumference towards an opening a quarter of the way around. It did not matter how deeply I breathed, how intently I focussed on the sounds, how often I thought about finding Strachan, or how carefully I stepped in the dark, I could not stem the flow of tears.

When I got to the gap in the circle, I saw a monk inside. He was sitting on one of 12 flat gabbro rocks protruding from the earth, which stuck out like low stools inside the boundary of green roses like a boardroom in the middle of nature. The rose bush clung to my sleeves like a child clutching its mother as I filled the entrance, looking into the face of the chanting monk. He sang a song so comforting yet incomprehensible. Such was the completeness of noise hitting me—a chorus of voices so deep and smooth—I could not believe that he was truly alone. He rose purposefully from his gabbro perch and looked deep into my runny eyes.

"Come in," said the monk, calmly, while gesturing for me to enter. "Pain brings everyone here, eventually. Welcome to Killaby."

My eye muscles tightened with suspicion.

"Where is he?" I barked at him. "Where is Strachan?"

"What brings you here?" the monk replied, still speaking in a sweet, silky voice.

"Yes, I—" I broke off for a moment as he started towards me, "—I am here to get to the truth, to confront the man who is somewhere around here. Where is he?"

"Ah yes, the truth…" he said thoughtfully, "…and what lies beneath, isn't it?" he stopped a metre just before me and went on staring. "Do you know where you are?"

"This is Kill—"

"—illaby?" the monk finished it for me. "Of course, you would say that. But this is more than just a mountain, Leo."

"I figured as much, that is why I am here—to find out. Along with what it has to do with Citizen Science," I said.

The monk laughed knowingly to himself. "Well, everyone has their reasons."

"What is yours?" I was a little annoyed but also curious.

"I am the guardian of Killaby. Come in, sit down, I'll tell you what you need to know."

"I'm good here," I said, sniffling a little. "Go on. Guardian…?"

"This is a very special mountain," he continued, always choosing his words carefully. "One of seven on the planet, each with their own guardian. Here on Killaby, the monastery has provided guardians for over a thousand years. Long before the Days of Fire, before the Leidenturians and long before…" he stopped. "The point is, my friend, that once a monk is given his mission, it becomes his mission for life. And mine is to protect Killaby from those who might want to misuse its power, and to serve those who are sent to it—people like you." He paused for a few moments, as if allowing me the time to soak it in. Even with that allowance, nothing made sense to me. He must have seen the absence on my face.

"Everything here is perfectly placed, Leo. *Nothing* happening here is accidental," he sat back on his words, only speaking when he felt them. "What do you think brought you here, at this time? Within this mountain lies a certain power, a power beyond that of physical life, what you can describe as a portal, if you like, and which, just by being in its presence, here, where we stand, helps to facilitate change in you. Just being here right now is significant. Do you see? Like I say, you are not here accidentally. Many have tried but few are able to stand where you are, right here, until they are ready."

"Right," I mocked. "So you are saying I'm here because I'm ready?"

"Well, you are here, after all."

"What am I ready for? And this portal, where does the portal take you?"

"You must crawl before you can walk, my friend," said the monk. "Just know that it is helping me to help you."

"Perhaps, then, you can help me find Ray Strachan, the Chancellor of Philomena. He is here somewhere, and it must be this portal that he is after."

I had a warm feeling that I was beginning to uncover something at last. The monk laughed knowingly again and started towards me. His hooded robe dangled gracefully at his feet, dark green and heavy-looking, covering him like a duck cloth raincoat.

"And what do you seek, Leo?"

He was upon me before I could answer, raising his right hand toward my left shoulder. I lurched to my right and he stretched over me to break off one of the roses from the bush. He brought his arm back with the flower in his grip and held it closely in front of me. I smelt Sasha's perfume.

"The answers are right in front of you, Leo."

Sasha came rushing back to my mind, pulling my attention away from the monk's timeless black skin and striking green eyes. I saw her as she was the morning we met on the bus to school. We were sitting in the back of a 12-seater minivan. Hurricane season brought frequent storms to Divitia that year, and the heavy morning showers forced us to close all of the windows in the van. It was an oven inside. I was sweating buckets when I caught Sasha looking at me from the corner of her eye, sniggering bashfully, and teasing with flirty flicks of her braids. She pulled out some tissues from her school bag and offered them to me. "Here take this," she said. I was as embarrassed as I was grateful.

"Hot isn't it?" I said with as much machismo as I could find.

"It is for you, obviously," she replied, her lips quivering under the disguise of seriousness. It was funny to her that I was sweating twice as much as anyone else. Her eyes said something different though. They were smiling, tinted with adoration. We spoke with basic conversation that you would expect from two teens on a school bus, but her eyes spoke in the ageless language of love. I guessed my own eyes were glowing with the same soul-desire.

That flash of a memory lasted a long time. The monk waited patiently on me as I thought about how young Sasha and I were when we got married and started a family. Life was kind to us—a comfortable house for our growing family and spare money in the bank. When Divitia felt too small, we travelled. First by exploring parts of Divitia that we could only dream of as teenagers, then visiting the gems of Amplaviridi and further afield in other parts of the world. We created a long but well thought-out list of destinations—not on paper, but written in our collective mind by the invisible matrimonial hand that guided our lives.

A scurrying sound in the mountain behind me pushed Sasha into retreat again. I wanted to look around, but I was frozen in position, debilitated by a torrent of feelings. Irritation, depression, powerlessness, anxiety, desperation, frustration, bitterness, resentment, flowed around my body and, with idea that Strachan was at last presenting himself—rage. The monk retreated into the darkness, his robes barely visible against the backdrop of green.

"You shouldn't have come here!" shouted Strachan.

His voice slow and heavy as I heard him unzipping something, generating a grating noise like a sword coming out of its sheath. I felt him behind me. The master of illusion took advantage of my disembodiment that came with memories of Sasha. A blow came down on the back of my neck that stunned me. There was no pain, just a floppy feeling in my knees which were already wobbling gelatinously. Everything morphed into blinding white light, then dimmed slowly and then it was back to black.

CHAPTER 20

I regained consciousness as a bear would emerge from hibernation. Strachan was talking aloud to himself, kind of like a rehearsal for an upcoming play.

"There is no difference between you and me. You are here for solutions, I am here for solutions," Strachan said in a less agitated voice.

Getting back to my feet, I saw him taking things out of his bag and setting up a camp of some kind in the centre of the gabbro seats. He talked as he worked, giving me the occasional glance. His confidence surprised me, the freedom with which he operated, no longer perturbed by my presence. I quickly realised it was because my hands were tied. I must have been out for hours. I wondered where the monk had gone, and why he would leave me at such a time.

"I thought you were the guardian on Killaby!" I shouted into space, like a wolf howling to the moon.

Strachan dropped what he was holding and looked

at me. "Guardian? No, no, you must be mistaken. I am no guardian—I am a scientist, and you are witnessing history. Consider yourself lucky, eh?"

"I know about the portal, Ray," I said, stumbling towards him.

He lowered his head and nodded grimly. "You are one annoyingly persistent fellow. So, what now?" he said, edging towards his bag.

Three long black rods had already been inserted into the ground in the centre. There was another in his hand. I could not see how many remained.

"The portal, I know about it," I told him again, my voice weakened.

Strachan froze in his tracks. "Have you ever heard that expression—it's better to have loved and lost than to never have loved before?"

I thought about Sasha before I replied, "I'm not sure I have. Why don't you tell me what you mean and what this has to do with all of this?" I replied with a smirk.

"Don't you patronise me, boy," his voice boomed just as lightning snaked across the sky.

Outside of the green rose circle the storm grew stronger, the atmosphere released little balls of light which spontaneously appeared in the space around. I looked on in astonishment.

"Sprites," he said. "The rarest of all known lightning phenomena. Beautiful, aren't they?" He said, then his voice became gravelly. "Extremely rare phenomena, and so, so precious—just like my Clara. Do you know what it is to lose someone, Leo?"

"I—"

"Don't interrupt me!" he shouted, his bulbous nose wrinkled with irritation. Then he went on, "Let me tell you a story, Leo." He spoke in a slow and careful tone. "My great, great grandfather owned a mine on one of your neighbouring islands. Those were the glorious days when Leidenturia dominated the world. When my forefathers first came to these Amplaviridian shores, there was profit potential beyond their wildest dreams. But there were snakes here which brought the prospect of terror and the loss of man manpower—and therefore productivity—from snake bites."

Strachan walk around his bag as he spoke, his eyes jumping between back-and-forth movements and a looking at the sticks he placed in the ground. He shot a rapid glance at me when I wriggled hoping to get some relief from the cables ties cutting into my wrists.

"So what happened to the people?" I said, refocussing his mind. "Because the mines continued to churn out billions since then."

"Oh, I'm getting there," he said. "To deal with this little snake problem, a small population of mongooses from the Eastern subcontinent were brought over. It should be no surprise to you that profits, the mines – especially the RMC—and what you call 'foreign invaders' like me, are still part in the DNA of the system Divitians live so quietly under today. Anyway, those magnificent creatures were so adept at killing snakes of almost any kind that, before long, the mongooses rendered the entire snake population extinct while their own number thrived."

My hands slid around tied behind my back when—lubricated by the blood dribbling from cuts in my wrists—I freed myself from the ties. Plus, I was growing tired of the monologue.

"What has this to do with Killaby?" I asked again, but he just went on, as if enraptured by his own floridity.

"Those little bastards had no natural predators in this new eco-system of course, so they reproduced until their number doubled that of the human population. That brought its own problems—damage to property, crops and livestock. Traps. The people made traps, Leo. After capturing thousands of these things and harvesting them for their fur, there were only two left, a single pair, one male, one female. They became known locally as the Matriarch and the Patriarch and their lives were spared. You see, Leo, when mongooses find their perfect love, they stay together—it's in their nature. But these two mongooses were separated when my grandfather kept the female and put the male back into the wild. So, the male mongoose, having lost his mate, his *soulmate*, stopped at nothing to find her, Leo. At nothing! The havoc he wreaked in pursuit of his love was boundless. He had his freedom, but he was not truly free. Not until he found her. That little mongoose continued untiringly and was willing to do anything—*everything*—to get back to his love. Even if it meant death."

"Stop fucking with me Ray," I said, exasperated. The man was bordering on lunacy.

Strachan raised his voice. "He never found her, but he was willing to move mountains to do so. So, you can call me the Patriarch, and I am willing to do the same for my Matriarch, even if that mountain is Killaby."

Strachan bent over for his backpack, put the rod in

his hand back inside and hurried away. I tried to move quickly through the circle in pursuit, but my body was still weak, wet and cold from lying unconscious. I laboured through the centre of gabbro rocks to the opposite side of the circle to find another gap in the hedge hidden by the rain and the darkness, through which Strachan had disappeared into the night.

CHAPTER 21

I looked at the monk with an undisguisable weariness, he looked at me meekly. My eyeballs were the only part of my body that moved without restriction, so I cast them up and down his robes, and met him back in his glowing eyes. They looked right through me.

"You let him get away!" I said.

"Still you seek, but still you don't find. Do you not consider that strange?" He smiled less this time.

"I could have used your help before you let him get away," I said in a feeble but impatient voice.

"The mountain hides nothing if you know where to look. Let me help you, Leo."

"That's what I've been asking for, help me find him."

"Leo, you have your job and I have mine," he said, then waited a moment for his comment to settle in my mind. He came forward again, reaching to place his hand on my shoulder. "Why do you still weep, Leo?"

"I am inches away from truth now, I can taste it. Strachan wants to use the portal for something to do with his dead wife. And he seems to think he can bring her back—or something, I don't know."

"I told you Killaby was a special place did I not? So many have come here to face their demons, so many that, in my tenure alone, I have lost count. And yet you do not know why you are here. Tell me," he said, pulling his hand back to his side, "why do you still weep?"

I was drenched and it was dark. *There is no way he can see my tears,* I thought.

"I don't need to see your tears to feel your pain," he said, as if reading my mind. "What pains you?"

My attention scattered into many pieces, broken into parts with reflections of Strachan, Philomena, Ana, Citizen Science—

"Fool yourself no longer, Leo," said the monk, breaking my thought pattern again.

I relented almost involuntarily. Not quite like being forced, rather the outpouring came of its own volition. First, I lamented Jamal. I recounted our life together growing up. I told the monk about our friendship—

about school, broken bones, brotherhood, the gang, the jokes, the Rum Shack, J's loyalty, patience, his wisdom. I did not stop there. I went on about his mother, how his father was like my father, and the tragedy of his death.

The monk's face was lit up by light from passing sprites, like little soap bubbles bursting into existence out of nothing and then floating away. They were rare, yet seemed unremarkable, possibly due to my fatigue, my being lost in my words and being drawn in by the depth of his expressionless face, which was somehow warming, immobile yet concerned. His eyes showed me things in them—a TV screen of pulsating shapes that I had seen in my dream with Frasier. I heard the same sounds too, only clearer. The sound of whales turning into the voices of my Dante, Eli and Sasha, singing the lullaby she sang to them nightly.

The moving pictures eventually died down in his eyes, like the fading-to-black of a movie at the end of the credits, and revealed a depth of a galactic quality. My clenched hands were—to my feelings—like a collapsing dam to a large river. I was still talking all that time, not realising when I moved on from speaking about J to crying about Sasha.

"…and the years went by just like that. I mean, we ran our home like a well-oiled machine, you know? The bills were met, the kids got to school and back on time—it was clockwork. Then one day, for reasons I can only guess, she just left me."

"You are grieving, my friend," the monk said. "Yet you remain so unaware—"

I spoke over him, becoming more emotional then, weeping and convulsing like a small child.

"…I don't know what was missing between us, maybe life got in the way of living. I mean, quality time is important, you know? We talked about everything—literally everything—except us. We never talked about our own problems, which stayed under the carpet somewhere and it spilled out eventually, messing up everything. We looked perfect to everyone. Family lunches on Sunday were good. We led busy lives independently, but we made sure every Sunday we sat together—but I'm here and she is wherever. You know once, she asked me if I wanted to have another baby. I don't remember answering because I thought it was a joke."

I covered my face then. The reflex of shame, disappointment, anger, and regret took command of my arms. "I should have paid more attention," I muffled through my palms. "Eventually, the fire she wanted to feel wasn't one I could offer her, or least one she didn't think I could offer. She sought it elsewhere, both in experiences and people. I guess I trundled along like the zombie I had become, to the cliff edge of failure, while she went into the arms of another."

The monk stood beside me then to offer a gesture of comfort as I folded over, my arms around my stomach, hugging myself and retching from the agony. I did not recognise the wailing coming from my own mouth. He then placed his warm palm on my upper back between my shoulder blades. It felt good.

"Acknowledging your grief is a good start. Self-honesty, yes, but do not wallow in self-pity, my friend."

"But I've lost everything!"

"Have you lost *everything*?" he asked.

"Every fucking thing!"

"Your anger is misplaced, Leo," explained the monk, before taking a deliberate pause.

I sniffled on like a small, lost boy bawling in a fairground, when it was time to go home.

"Let us walk, Leo," he said, leading me away from the circle. We paced slowly back into the windy darkness outside of the hedges. I heard the plop-plop sound of puddles which showed themselves briefly under flashes in the sky. The sprites did not venture outside of the hedge, seemingly tethered to the middle of the monk's council.

"Now that you have begun to let yourself feel," the monk continued, "you must also allow yourself to grieve. Know that you will move faster through this stage by accepting it. We men have suffered this problem of denial for centuries, conditioned by systems of thinking that perpetuate suffering. We run from our own feelings and fear being perceived as weak. I hope you can see that this is not helpful. Emotions are normal and constantly in a state of flux. See them as energy in motion—it will serve you well. Remember that energy can neither be created nor destroyed, only transformed. If you don't let this energy flow through you, it will turn into disease. Is that what you want for yourself?"

"Well, if I didn't allow this to happen, I wouldn't have to worry about this. I wasn't good enough."

"Ah, guilt—the manifestation of self-loathing. Why must you beat yourself up in this way? Simply acknowledge the feeling, and let it be. Can you do that?"

"How will that get me my life back? Huh? Jamal is gone, Sasha is gone, the kids are gone. How will 'acknowledging' bring back what I had?"

"The past is gone, Leo, all you have is *now*."

"Now? Well, now there is nothing. She has reduced me to ashes. There will be no phoenix rising, I assure you."

"Does that make you feel good, Leo? Does it make you feel good to play the victim? Where is the pay-off? You must be getting some satisfaction from playing this role to cling to it this way."

His words stoked my anger again. I had no answer for him but I complained as I did before. "I miss my kids. I miss my life. Citizen Science is the only thing I've got."

"Wake up, Leo!" He said firmly. It was as though I'd been sent to the headmaster's office for a dressing-down. "And what after Citizen Science? Your experiences are dictated by your own consciousness. If you start by changing the habit pattern you are in, your experiences will also change. You are solely responsible for where you are. No one else. And you must be prepared to accept this."

My chin rose from its familiar groove on my chest as he continued. It was a sermon of sorts, without the preachiness. He spoke gently, though there was no doubting the conviction.

"It is time you take ownership of your feelings and actions. You can be a cause or you can be an effect—ownership or victimhood."

"But…"

"Ownership? Or victimhood?"

"Ownership," I said in a muffled gurgling voice as if talking underwater.

"There is no shame here, my friend. Shame just creates more shame. These are things you must respect, not empower. Respect them like you would a beast of nature, appreciate that it is there and that it has a role to play in life, but don't invite it to set up home in your house. That wouldn't be good for you."

I wish you would shut the hell up, I thought.

"I see that your anger rises. Anger can be good, if you learn how to harness that energy and put it to good use."

Like toward dealing with Strachan.

"You may, if you wish, dwell in hatred though that will not help you either."

"I don't hate him," I said, "nor Sasha, nor anyone else. Even if I have blown a fuse every now and then." My body warmed and became more fluid, in addition to analgesic effect of anger moving through me.

"Anger is better than apathy. Self-directed anger is self-abuse. Transmutation is the key and if you are mindful, Leo, you will be able to move through these phases of pain even faster."

A ruffling in the circle interrupted us. We were not quite side by side—he was a little ahead when I stopped to peer within the circle. In the corner of my eye, I saw the monk ambling onwards, unaware that I had stopped. My concern about that dangling conversation was small in comparison to the bigger fish I had on a hook. Strachan had questions to answer.

"You don't give up do you?" said Strachan as I entered, "You are like a little cockroach that refuses to die."

"I won't die without the truth," I replied.

"You are here now, Leo, so you may watch the truth with your own two eyes." Strachan mumbled to himself while he triggered the cylinders at the heart of the portal with a handheld device.

"Who is working with you on this portal project?"

I asked, shouting over the hissing and buzzing noises of something firing up. "I know you have backers here in Divitia. Who are they? And what do they want with the portal?"

"I don't care what they want! I want what *I want*. And that is that Clara and I will be reunited at last."

A whirring sound took over the monk's council as a turbine warmed up, letting off bright electrical discharges in between the poles in the ground. They competed with blue-white flashes of lightning, forming a triangular shape of electricity. I began to see his blatant lunacy for what it was. He used them all—Philomena, the HOIB, even his own daughter—to fulfil his fantasy.

"You can't bring Clara back to life, Ray, such things are not possible I'm afraid," I told him.

"Ah, so you aren't that knowledgeable after all. I overestimated you, Leo. Do you not know the power this mountain holds to put broken hearts back together? The gift of access it grants to other universes, places, times? I must confess to you, I am not sure which place or time yet either, but I know this mountain is special. It holds the potential to rid the Earth of all pain and suffering. Down there…" exhorted Strachan, raising his finger and pointing towards the black lowlands of Eastmoor, "…they only care about the power that the control of the portal will grant them. They want this portal so that they can wield the power of Gods over you. I admit, Leo, I care little for all of that. The idea of being seen as a saviour of men holds no sway over me. I am now freed of the shackles of such aims, free of the obsession to be the first to proclaim spaciotemporal dominance—" Strachan broke off and lowered his head. "Leo," he said feebly, "I just want to see my Clara again, that's all."

Only then did I see him as he was, with his naked insanity, controlled by the talons of grief. He had hidden himself so well until that moment.

"Ray," I said, taking careful steps forward. "What about Ana? What about Divitia? Have you no worries about their fate? You have no idea what repercussions your actions may bring."

"Have you ever known the animals of the plain to celebrate wildfire? Or joy at lands lost to the lava of a volcano? Do not see this as probable annihilation, Leo, but as creative destruction. For something to be born, something must die," he pointed toward the currents, "and this is the doorway to the new."

Against the astonishing electrical light fizzing in the centre, Strachan's body looked a silhouette. He moved backwards deliberately then, as if handling something with great care. "This is the final hurdle here, Leo. Why should I tell you the truth with my mouth, when you can see it with your own eyes?"

I felt Strachan slipping away, and with him, the whole reason for Citizen Science. Keeping him talking yielded everything but the truth. He only spoke statements coloured with grief, pain and delusion.

"She was the most precious thing, you know, the most precious thing," he mumbled to himself, as though sinking into drunkenness. "And she is dead because of me. Because of *me*! It was an accident, Leo. But it was my fault. My fault. It was all my fault." He wept.

"Tell me, Ray," I approached slowly. "Why? Why all of this? Why not another way?"

"Stop there," he said, pushing his hand out at me. "No closer, stop there, no closer!"

He paused, staring into the electric currents as one would look into a fireplace. His nose was more prominent then, exaggerated by the upward angle of the buzzing light. His eye sockets looked sunken into dark caves created by the shadows of his cheek bones. Even in the dark he could not hide his whiteness, contrasting even more against the black lines in the corner of his eyes and mouth. I stopped short of his hand, which he dropped, letting it fall into a swing like a pendulum. Strachan began to talk again, his voice croakier, his words more fluid.

"It was back in Leidenturia when I lost her. We were part of a top-secret research project tasked with investigating the portal in the Alps of Ventura. The powers-that-be felt that cracking this portal would allow us to master the elements—at the very least, provide the key to developing teleportation. Do you understand the significance of such a discovery? And how that would strengthen the hand of the puppet masters? The spectrums of dominance would be complete." He paused as though waiting for me to answer. "You wouldn't understand, I suppose," he continued, "you're Divitian after all. Anyway, my Clara—rest her soul—was my partner on this project and she made a discovery which ignited a scepticism in her that surprised me.

"The power could be misused," I said, recalling the monk's mission.

"Let's just say it scared her," said Strachan. "Yet

the potential of the discovery was so significant, I felt it was worth the risk. No one knows the pain I have carried with me over the years, or what I have given for my work. The sacrifices and burdens. I'm the one to blame. So, I am going to put it right. And I will do so with Clara's own discovery. Now, I bet you're wondering what Clara discovered, aren't you?" He paused again in anticipation of a reply.

I said nothing but I felt his words charging through my body like a bull on fire. Strachan began to look human. His eyes remained settled absently on the electricity lighting up the inner circle as he went on.

"Clara discovered the portal's power, not just to transcend space, but also time, Leo. Her heart was so pure that she felt that it was wrong. She thought that if we had the power to change the past, then we would warp the fabric of natural order. But I was adamant that we continued, and I convinced her that we should keep the discovery to ourselves. I took the work even further, insisting that we conduct our own 'parallel program of research', if you like. But my Clara was right all along. She warned me and I didn't listen. Listen, take this example, Leo. The first time Clara used the portal to travel in time, she saw that we would struggle to have our own children. So, we adopted Ana. Now, you can see, Clara is no longer with us. Three days before she died, Clara woke up screaming from a nightmare. She looked at me and said, 'Ray, we are on the wrong path, we must stop this right now. Please honey, we must!' I was enraged by her suggestion and I yelled at her to drop it," he said.

Strachan went silent and his face scrunched, as though the memory had become too heavy for him. "And would you believe it? I never found out what she dreamt." Strachan looked to the floor and nodded in disappointment, "I never found out what she dreamt. Then, on that fateful day, we wandered down to the research facility under the mountain. We knew that we would be alone". He stopped abruptly and let out a weak whimper. "That was when it happened."

He raised his head, and looked around with suspicion, as if he felt he had said too much. The lines on his face, seemingly drawn by the hand of misery, were etched deeper, carrying his tears like an estuary. He stepped back, returning to the gap in the roses and quickly disappeared behind the curtain of raindrops. In almost the same instant the monk reappeared behind me and rested his arm upon my left shoulder.

"Why do you still weep, my friend? I have watched you suffer long enough," he said.

Any words that came to mind became wedged in my throat. I did not realise I was still crying. Attention was all that I needed to make them come—betrayal, jealousy and rejection poured freely from my body until I was fully submerged.

The monk pivoted me around my shoulder and held me like a father would his son. "You are steaming hot, my friend," he said, "let this grief consume you no longer."

He put his hand on my shiny head and held me up with his other arm which was wrapped around my torso. What strength was left in my knees gave way to my desire to be held. I was tired of sobbing intractably, so I stopped resisting him and I let him hold me—I needed him to hold me. For that instant, no matter how close I was to solving the Citizen Science smoke screen—and how much Strachan's pining for Clara was driven by insanity—I felt different.

"You are ready to move beyond anger now. You must go towards forgiveness, compassion, and love. *That* is what Killaby is all about, my friend. That is why you are here." The monk's voice soothed me.

"You told me to put my anger to good use—that is what I am doing. Even if Strachan doesn't come clean, he is definitely on course to cause us harm."

"I'm not talking about whoever, Leo, I'm talking about you. Let me worry about the portal," he said. "That's my role here. You are still carrying so much. Let it go now. Let the love that is already inside of you flow, for that is the true victory. Love is the beginning and the end, the all-knowing, all-healing and the freeing essence. It can transcend all boundaries and ills if you let it."

"But I loved her. I loved Sasha, that was true love. And how far did that get me?"

"Ah," he said, with an air of satisfaction. "So now you speak the truth. It is not the man, after all—the one you call the chancellor—that is really troubling you?"

I began to take my own weight as the monk released me from his grip. "Maybe it is about her."

"Closer," he said with a smile.

I looked at him, awaiting an explanation.

"It is really about you," he said.

"Ah yes," I said, "I see now, it's about me and my love for her."

The monk nodded his head. "Do not conflate love

with attachment, Leo. The desire to hold on to what once was because of what it gave *you* is the epitome of attachment. Now, I'm not saying that you don't love your Sasha, but pure love has nothing to do with your wants. True love is independent of your needs. True love has no conditions."

"But she—"

"Leo," he stopped me in my tracks. "We are not talking about anyone else here anymore. Can you not see how stuck you have become? Stuck in your expectations of her? Or, this chancellor person you refer to? You want her to be the way *you* want her to be, rather than seeing her the way she is."

"She expects things of me also!" I protested.

"Perhaps. But recognise that love in that instance is conditional. If your love depends upon that person meeting your expectation then, as I explained, it is not true love. True love is characterised by the absence of ulterior motives. There is no secret diary or records to refer to in future arguments. True love is characterised by wishing only the best for her, reflecting the knowledge that what you wish for others you ultimately wish for yourself. Now I know that somewhere inside of you, you understand this and are ready to forgive and let go.

That is why you are here."

"I have already forgiven all that I need to forgive. I am on Killaby for Strachan, and the truth."

"You wouldn't know the truth if it came up here, sat down next to you, and looked you in the eye my friend. Forgiveness does not happen overnight. It is a continuous process, Leo, not a single event. The more pertinent question is, have you forgiven yourself?"

My entire relationship with Sasha flickered before my eyes. I saw her gleaming as she held our first-born son, so radiant that all around basked in her glow. A glimmer of warmth filled me, in contrast to the focus on what I had lost. If my body had not been squeezed so tightly by anger and sorrow for so long, I might have smiled. The impulse was certainly there, but the manifestation was another matter.

"You are beginning to see now, my friend," he stopped and touched the centre of my chest with his finger, "that *that* is love." He spoke unconcerned by the popping sound of the Strachan's probes behind him. He made a couple of steps toward his gabbro perch and invited me to sit.

"I prefer to stand," I said.

"Compassion," said the monk, fixing his robes

around him as he sat, "is a metamorphizing agent, an ingredient that can change the course of history. It takes only a small act of compassion to save an entire species. Did you know that the Fresden Dragon was almost extinct?

I wanted to answer with a "no, I didn't," but I didn't need to because he carried on without missing a breath.

"Almost three hundred years ago, when I started my tenure as guardian, the modern colonisers hunted the dragons for trophies, such was their ignorance. Unfortunately, it was a past-time that did not die with them; it was inherited by the free people of Divitia after the Days of Fire. One day, while leading a hunting party right here on Killaby, the man now known as the father of Divitia, Andrew Barrington, shot a dragon through the trees. When he excitedly ran to collect his trophy, he discovered a baby Fresden wailing in distress. Now, bear in mind, my friend, that Andrew was an experienced hunter, however there was something different about that day. It was the day that Andrew saw that, as aggressive and territorial as the dragons are known to be, those poor creatures can suffer too. A window of compassion opened in Andrew that completely transformed the face of Divitia. It was the last day he hunted the Dragon and shortly afterwards he led a motion through parliament that made hunting of Fresden Dragons a crime. A year after that, he honoured the Fresden by making it the official animal of Divitia. That is the true story of the origins of the Day of the Fresden."

As his words came to an end, the turbine noises from Strachan's apparatus in the centre livened. The electric currents got brighter, turning from brilliant blue to crisp white flickers dancing like birds on a wire. Strachan returned, without an utterance, apparently consumed by himself.

I looked at the monk and sighed in quiet recognition. The resolution was that a space was opening inside of me, twinkling like the first ray of sunlight over the horizon. I felt a gradual deflation in my chest, like air slowly discharging from a balloon. The monk watched on in silence as I came to terms with a catalogue of truths. He nodded, then flicked his robes away from his feet and slowly rose from the gabbro, glancing at me once more with his glowing eyes, as if wishing me good luck, before disappearing into the cover of Killaby.

CHAPTER 22

Stability came back to my legs I stood from the seat at the monk's council.

"Ray, it's time to stop this now."

Ray came back with nothing and proceeded as though he was alone. He made grumbling sounds between breaths, directed in all directions, and his words were almost always unintelligible. A dial in his left hand that shone in the light from a phone-sized screen above it and took the bulk of his attention, the rest of it went to something else outside the circle that appeared to be connected.

"Ray, this is the end of the road."

"Stay away, boy" he mumbled. "This is the end of the road, and it is between me and my Clara, not you. I have already told you all that you will get from me. If you want to know more, then you just have to watch."

"What about the project, and all the Citizen Scientists out there who have a stake in this? Won't they want to know the findings? What about Ana?"

"It's too late for them now. Reality as we know it will be forever changed if this goes the way I expect it to," said Strachan. "As for Ana, she will be just fine."

I walked towards him without a clue as to what I would do when I got there. Five seats at each side of the monk's council separated us, around which I moved crab-like, facing the portal doorway. Strachan was unaware of my motion towards him, blinded by his dream that I felt was certain to fail.

A long lightning strike brightened the sky and gave up his position, causing him to shoot up in a panic. He jumped backward. "Stop there!" He said, drawing a knife from his waist. "I promise you, boy, this will not end well for you."

I too stood back and showed him my hands, stuck out and up in the air in surrender. "There is no need for that," I said, nodding to the knife's tip glistening in the rain. "Let's just talk this out."

"We've done enough talking," he said, steam now rising off his body. "You could have had the whole library to yourself back in Westmoor, you could have married my daughter and had a life of bliss, but no, you chose to come here and stop me from completing my life's mission."

"Your library would have given me nothing about your true intentions, far less the intentions of the HOIB and whoever else out there seeks this portal," I said.

"I don't care what you want, Leo, and right now," he said, looking at his knife, "you are in no position to make demands."

Thunder clapped at will then, shaking the water out of the trees and presenting me with small opportunities to disarm him. "You are right," I said, "I will go."

When the thunder came, my body sprung through the air, coming down on his right arm up with a chopping motion. He yelped and the knife flashed as it fell to the ground. I fell to the ground after it. I landed elbow first with a thud that almost knocked me unconscious again. For a brief period, the zaps of light ripping across the sky reflected off the blade and I closed my eyes. My skull rattled with the impact but I had the knife, and that was all that mattered. By the time I got to my feet, Strachan could have been anywhere, but I was confident he would not have strayed too far from the portal.

Back on the outside of the hedge I stood in wait for his return. But Strachan was a smart man.

"Raymond Strachan!" I screamed. "Chancellor of Philomena, your Clara awaits you!" I waited for his reply and squinted in the darkness looking out for any turbulence in the bush. All I got was the white noise of rain falling on the leaves. I moved away from the monk's council behind me, with the gateway at the centre ablaze with the currents from Ray's equipment and the sprites giving lightshow to rival the best fireworks anywhere in Divitia. It lit the path ahead leading into the darkness on one of the four cardinal points from the circle.

Get off my mountain, boy!" his voice came out of the wood.

I felt a strange closeness to Ray. I understood his pain. Yet, while I was beginning to accept that he was beyond reason, I still attempted to lure him.

"Shame on your defiance of reality, Ray. You are no longer in a position to make such demands. Better that you come out and talk!" I shouted back.

The damp wood absorbed the sound, so I could not tell from which direction his voice came. In any case, the sound could not travel far. Apprehension widened my eyes more than the darkness and narrowed my focus only to what was in front of me. Scuffling sounds came from above me, which I thought were monkeys in the trees until the dead weight of Strachan hit the ground behind me with a thud. I swung around with arms out to shield myself from the blow I thought would follow. Instead, I met the patter of his boots running back to the circle and his dark outline moving away.

I followed him back to the circle, each of my strides boosted by an explosion of adrenaline. He was fast, and arrived with enough of a head start to have opened the gateway in the circle by the time I caught up.

Clara, my love. I am coming at last," he cried.

Back to where we started, I thought. My legs started to shake again as I faced the heat of the inner circle. I was sure he heard my heart pounding before I appeared. "Ray," I spoke, softly then, "let's end this."

"This is the end, Leo. All that remains is for me to open the door. I've done it. What went wrong in Ventura won't happen again. All we needed was Nephrite to bridge the different worlds and thanks to Killaby, I have loads of it."

Strachan reached into his bag for the cylindrical probe and connected himself to it with cables. He moved toward the currents. "Oh, and Leo, I am not bringing her back to me," he looked at me and grinned,

"I am going to her."

He inserted the probe into the flow of current, triggering a fountain of sparks that flew in all directions. He let out a high-pitched cry which sent shockwaves across the mountain mixed with care-free laugh that sliced open a wound of fear deep inside of me. A wretched sound so torturous, it was impossible to block out no matter how hard I pressed my hands to my ears. Screeching came from the sparkling portal as it threw particles like pellets from a grenade.

I remembered the large stones on the clearing outside of the hedge and set off in that direction, crawling on all fours away from the furnace. When I got to the rose circle, I looked over my shoulder at him. He screamed in pain from the intensifying heat which lit his eyes to the red glow that I saw back in the basement library. His horns showed too, outlined against the gateway like the silhouette of a bird flying in front of the sun. His pungent odour filled the air while his charcoal skin hissed, blistering and popping like small water balloons. Not even the sprites were visible in front of that blinding light.

It took a violent effort to get to my feet and run for cover behind the stone. Whooshing winds generated by the currents quickened to a steady buzz. Tucked behind the stone, I watched the portal gateway spark ferociously, spitting hot beams of light like lasers in all directions. Looking up to the heavens, Ray squealed, wept, laughed, and howled all at once. There was a raucousness to this episode. Watching him suffer in pain and simultaneously celebrate his liberation stretched my mind to delirium. Through the slits in my eyes, the electrical arcing spiralled and superheated the air until the stone that protected me broiled and became a threat in itself. I edged back to more distant cover and watched on in disbelief. Then, just as quickly as everything started, it came to a stop.

It went quiet. Cooked green roses sweetened the air with hints of honey and metal. There was a remnant afterglow in the circle, where countless sprites were still spinning, floating over the gabbro rocks where the monk sat. They spiralled, twinkling, like stardust in the galaxy. The wind was gone, so was the rain, no crickets, no night owls, no frogs, no fireflies—nothing but high-pitched ringing in my ears.

CHAPTER 23

Birdsong heralded the breaking of dawn. I left the circle in tatters with Strachan's ashes laying spread among the cinders. My chest moved freely with each breath I took for the first time since I arrived on Killaby. The sadness I felt for Strachan on my descent to the monastery was outweighed by my sense of relief. As the cool breeze bathed my lungs, any remnant thoughts of Strachan's motives washed away with my breath. Rays of light shot down from the sky unhindered and brightened the path unfolding ahead. I thought of my mother and what I might say to her.

"Hello, son," she answered me. She sounded surprised. "You've grown!"

"Hey Mum," I replied. "There is a lot to tell, but also much to learn."

"I believe you! Reaching out to me like this tells me there were big shifts for you on Killaby," she said.

"I didn't get very far with Citizen Science, but

there are things I need to ask you and Dad about," I said. "It concerns the HOIB."

"I see," said Mother, in a tele-speak voice coloured by intrigue. "I'm not sure your father will want to leave his house for this, but I can be with you in a couple of days?"

"That'd be nice. But for now, I'll head back to the monastery for some rest. See you on Monday." Mother left. I knew it would be better to tell her about Strachan in person. I thought about Ana too, and about how I would muster the courage to tell her about her father. There was still time for me to consider those things.

On the way down, I noticed the dreaded footsteps of something approaching. Killaby had a way of making you face the things you feared most, so I was not surprised at the appearance of a large Fresden Dragon. It moved slowly in the warming air, caked in wet mud and waddling across my path with predatory supremacy. It turned westward and made its way directly toward me. Running would have been futile, even if I'd had the energy to do so. It looked at me through its multi-layered eyelids, blinking outward from the corners and cooing, a deep sound—somewhere between a growl and hiss. Draped with coarse body armour, it stood face to face with me, sniffing my cheek with its tongue like a snake. I touched it on the left side of its cool skull when it began to croon softly, bobbing its wide head in acceptance. It might have been nature acting through me, or my absence of fear that provoked this unusually friendly behaviour. It didn't matter—I let the mystery of Killaby work its magic. A few seconds of interaction passed like hours before the dragon gave me one final nod of approval and disappeared into greenery.

* * *

Two days later, I packed up and left my cabin. I must have missed the black book behind the cabin door when I arrived the first time around. "A gift," the monk at reception told me upon checkout. I recognised it; it was the same lightning book from my dreams. I shoved it into my bag along with clothes that should have gone into the bin, and a small piece of Nephrite from the circle.

I beat Mother to Eastmoor by a few hours and kept busy until she knocked at door. The way she squeezed me when I saw her more than compensated for the years—before she visited me at J's funeral days before—that I had not seen her in the flesh.

"I like what you've done with the place," she said.

"Cleanliness is next to Godliness—a wise woman once told me," I replied.

Mother smiled as we took seats in the lounge. We exchanged pleasantries and general updates. Then, when I asked about dad, I learned about his biography, which would "shed light on a lot of things," she said.

"How so? You think he'll say much about the HOIB?" I asked her.

"What do you know of the HOIB?" she asked. "There isn't much to say."

I told Mother about what happened on Killaby and recounted the dreams. I told her everything she had missed along the way and retold things I had already shared, for the sake of completeness.

"Son, your father tried to leave the Order many times, but once you are in at a certain level, you cannot really leave. He may still be a member, but—as far as I know—he has not attended any meetings for many, many years."

"Why did he want to leave?"

Mother exhaled as though she did not want to be having this conversation. "The HOIB was, and probably still is, keen to access and exploit certain higher powers. You know your father is a suspicious man with small things, imagine how he felt about them during his years in the government—but there was little he could do. You must understand that nothing is what it seems, Leo."

"I am beginning to see this now," I said, and reminded Mother of what I just experienced at the portal.

"The HOIB, the RMC, the Tribes of Ether. None of these groups are important, my son," she began to explain. "I want you to see that there are many entities seeking powers that they should not have—the HOIB is but one. They work in the shadows. Men, and only men, who seek to control the world. That's what the Days of Fire were all about."

"But," I interjected. "That's why I wanted to speak to Dad about this."

"You father would never speak of this, son. People dissapear when they speak out of turn."

"So, the HOIB wants to control the world…"

"But it can't be done."

"…and they would do this by controlling resources…"

"Yes."

"…and they believe that the portal will give them

the power that grants them total control?"

"Son," Mother sighed. "You are better served by focussing your attention where it really matters— within *yourself*, rather than on those matters which you cannot wholly control."

I then told Mother about the monk I met on Killaby and everything he told me about my catharsis. She smiled again, now with vindication.

"The true discovery of what lies beneath the surface is inside of you," she said. "Emotions are the doorway to the soul."

"Why did you not tell me any of this before? Before all the pain, before all the craziness with the gang, and J?"

"My son," she said patiently. "You can't force a flower to grow. It must spring up under the right conditions, voluntarily, without force from outside. Pain is part of the conditions for growth—it is helpful to you. Your journey cannot be dictated by anyone else. When you are ready to sprout, only then is help provided. That is the work of The Elders."

"Like the monk?"

"Perhaps. Elders come in many forms. They come in dreams, they come in ordinary life, they can even be people who you do not like. The Elders' role is quite simple—to encourage you to take the first steps on your journey to self-awakening. To some people, Elders come, and when those people's resistance is too strong, they can quite often go mad. That is the cost of forcing change before conditions are right."

Mother left me wading through an assemblage of thoughts, from the HOIB and what they might do next, to my own journey of growth and healing—all very important but less urgent than the question of Ana, and how I should tell about her father's death.

I felt sad when Mother left, but my mind was soon occupied by Strachan again, and the puzzle of Ana and how I would break the terrible news. I wondered if she missed me. Excluding her recent displays of self-absorption, I missed her some. The rest of the day passed that way, dipping in and out of various thoughts about her.

I lay on my bed staring into the ceiling that night. Ana and I had planned to meet the next day, so I prepared myself by doing nothing. If the Elders were really there to help, then I trusted that they would help me through this. The clock ticked on the wall and as I lay, a new thought door opened into one lingering idea;

it occurred to me that my mother could be an Elder herself.

I unclenched my jaws and hands and my face softened like jelly. I took a deep breath in and then deflated into a deep, long sleep and into a dream of a different sort.

CHAPTER 24

River Revelacion was a forty-five-minute walk south of Eastmoor. I took the usual back passages between the close-knit village houses, a route I had been taking since I was a little boy. I passed under the breadfruit tree behind Lenny's house and through the alley that ran parallel to the parade.

That morning, Eastmoor was as still as a photograph and not a soul was in sight. I went up the steps, fashioned out of the very earth where they stood, and in a southerly direction; the back entrance to the barber's went by in a flash. The alley put me out onto a pot-holed road that narrowed the closer it got to the river. Long and straight as an arrow, waves of heat were rising from it, distorting an otherwise crispy-clear picture.

I heard a trickle of running water along the route, which passed by a derelict school building that stood behind a rusting wire fence on my left. The grass was brown, and the playfield was covered in sand. It was a desolate place, familiar to me but missing any suggestions of inhabitancy.

Normally, I would feel the heat from the road scurrying past my face as it rose, and the pinch of jagged stones on the soles of my feet, but there was no pain, no discomfort. The smell of muddy clay baking in the sun intermingled with fishy smells from the gutters and wafted toward me. After that, there was nothing noteworthy around apart from the bleakness of the sparce land.

I arrived at the track to the river, where the landscape was more luscious. Bamboo lined the route where I would usually see old men getting drunk on homemade Babash, but they weren't there. The large rocks they often sat on marked the entrance to a small lavish garden. Its carpet-like grass was lined with flat river stones directing me to a little oasis. At no time had I ever felt more at home than there, at that moment.

Toward the end of the garden there were three steps that pulled my attention due to the brilliant white light that shined from beyond it. When I approached the light, the gradual shape of someone appeared. The figure became clearer with each step it took closer to me. I saw him then, bringing a sense of tranquillity and oneness. I continued toward him and by the last step I was able to see him up close. Strong, silent, naked, and standing erect—that man was me.

CHAPTER 25

When I woke from that dream, I felt no fear, no alarm, no urge to solve anything. It was primarily a day for celebration, the day I was born: July 24th.

Ana and I had arranged to meet later at the Lakes. I left the small problem—of not knowing how to give her the bad news of her father's death—to the moment itself. I was still digesting the circumstances of his self-destruction; it was pointless pre-planning the best way to explain the inexplicable. I got a text message from her, "Happy birthday, Leo! Can't wait to see you. No luck finding who was responsible for the break-in yet, but I am sure it will come out soon. See you at the Lakes. Can't wait x."

I thought I got to the Lakes early, but I was mistaken. "Happy birthday!" Ana shouted, jumping out from behind a tree. She wrapped her arms around me and gave me a coffee. "Divitian black for you, and a latte for me," she said, beaming. "How was your trip to the monastery? Able to process things?" Her crippling anxiety about her father's stolen book seemed to have dissolved, replaced by an elation at my return, like a child getting what they always wanted for Christmas.

"It was a good break," I said, equably.

"O—kay," she said, probably sensing something strange or perhaps wanting a similar display of excitement. "Let's walk and talk," she said. "Shall we go around the lake?"

"Yes, that'd be nice," I agreed.

"You seem different, Leo. I can't quite put my finger on it. Are you okay?"

"A lot has happened," I said.

"Good! I look forward to hearing all about it. Things are exciting for me right now. The Citizen program has found mind-blowing data, Leo—this is big, big news for the university. And it looks like our funders want to increase their support! My father would be so proud if he were here right now."

"Oh, wow, congratulations, Ana, I'm so happy for you. But about your father—"

"It's way too early to tell, but it looks like we are going to have to expand the research to include a broader range of possibilities!"

"Good, good," I said. "Ana, it's about you father—"

"Leo, let's just run away and get married, shall we?" Ana said happily. "Wait—" she stopped in her tracks, "What? What about my father, Leo?" Her tone dropped suddenly.

I paused for a second and pivoted around to face her, taking our coffees and placing them on the ground. Her hands went limp as I held them and looked her in the eyes. A wisp of her blonde hair blew in the wind coming off the lake which released that enchanting floral mist.

"What is it, Leo?"

"I'm really sorry, Ana, but—your father is dead."

Ana froze and stared off into the lake. Her face went sheet-white, her hands frigid. It was as if I had killed her myself. Short of actual death, she seemed to be lost in a reverie from which she could not be summoned. I thought I saw her lips quiver and her eyes dancing in step, but then she came back to herself and looked at me, first with horror and then with a gawk of bewilderment.

"Ana, I know. I'm sorry—" I put my arm around her.

"Leo," she interrupted, "my father has been dead

for over twenty years."

A long dead silence followed, broken only by the lapping water on the lake's edge and the gentle breeze passing through the trees.

***

That evening I sat on the sofa in my living room, in the same spot where Ana had left me. She wanted to stay to make sure I was alright, but I preferred to be alone. I sat with the book from the monastery in my hand and gaped at the piece of nephrite on the table beneath an old family painting of Killaby hanging on my wall. My father had received it as a gift exactly nine months before I was born, and he gave it to me when I first moved into that house. I had had it for years, but probably only *truly* saw it for the first time just then. Beautiful strokes of green and purple illuminated the sky and the forest adorning the surface of the mountain was almost silhouetted out. There was an energy, a glow, radiating off the mountain, which stepped out of the painting in that moment and hit me in the chest, as though the painting itself had come alive. It was signed: "the guardian."

I sunk into my chair and reflected on everything that happened to me in my entire life up until that juncture. I felt Jamal's presence as though he were right beside me. I considered how he came to see me the day before he died when he took me down to the parade. I also considered that all of these occurrences were interconnected somehow, and that the truth was always speaking inside of me—if only I had listened more.

It mattered not that the events of the past took place in a specific place and at a specific time—they all seemed to change with my current perspective as though my *present* was creating my past, right there and then, like a ship creating the waves in its wake. Many of the events had been perfectly orchestrated to get me to the next point in time. I wondered if somehow everyone in my life was an actor, and all the events a play in which the cast danced to the tune of something much greater, as though everything that conspired to get me onto Killaby to find the truth was no accident, but faultless and in absolute equilibrium. I opened the book from the monastery with the lightning strike embossed on the spine; it read simply: "Stroke of Insight."

I closed my eyes and smiled at the pictures in my mind of Sasha and the kids playing together as cherry blossoms blew in the cool breeze across my face. The aroma of cotton-fresh linen and damp earth pressed softly under bare feet. I stood before a wide-open field which rolled ahead for miles on end, and met the deep blue sky at the vanishing point of my eye. I inhaled deeply, and my taste buds came alive—the sweetness of it all, dancing on my tongue. I exhaled slowly as my cycle of breath died a beautiful death, only to do it all over again.

ACKNOWLEDGEMENTS

There was an expression that went, "when life gives you lemons, make lemonade." For me—and this book—that meant that when life gives you lessons, take them (even if they are acid!). I want to thank my mother for instilling those kinds of principles in me from a young age and for founding the Metaphysical Bookstore in the early 1980s. I also want to thank my sister Nicola for reading through this book over and over again. My father too—for his saint-like patience in helping me massage the text.

Thanks to Denise Harris for giving me the courage to get started with From Lost to Love, the genesis of this book. I continue to be fortunate to have a team of brothers by way of Stephen Marriott, Shack Baker and Brian O'Toole for being unshakeable soundboards for my ideas and to Simon Richardson and Keith Allden for helping me persevere through numerous drafts. Thanks must also go to Paul Gill, who's insistence on honing the craft for its own sake resulted in even more drafts! If there was no Ed Zhao, my early confidant and unwitting art advisor, there would be no map of Amplaviridi, Divitia, Makhzwane or any of the wonderfully depicted countries of this world. Thanks must also go to George Hadley for capturing the essence on the cover of the book and to Flora Snelson for tightening up my language and keeping me on the straight and narrow. Without the generosity of Roland Merullo, my release date might have been somewhere in the 2050s, while I built my confidence up.

Thanks to all who I may not have mentioned here but who I met along the way, who encouraged me to write—and to continue writing—and to my network of advisers and supporters.

ABOUT THE AUTHOR

Calvin Niles was born in the Caribbean Island of Barbados to a civil servant father and Trinidadian mother who was a homemaker, nurse and spiritual teacher. Growing up around meditation and metaphysical teachings planted certain seeds in him from a young age. Those seeds began to sprout much later in his life while living in the United Kingdom where he lived a typical life of work, family and career. When the foundations of his relationships and a colourful portfolio career began to shake, he learned there was much more to life than the pursuit of ordinary things. A complete reorientation of his life ensued, toward emotional healing and personal growth, and serving others through coaching, writing and teaching. That journey inspired him to write the story of Eastmoor, the first in a series of fiction books.

Are the events of our lives mostly determined by our perspectives?

See how your lens of perception can change through exploring true stories of the author's life and how he has chosen to interpret them.

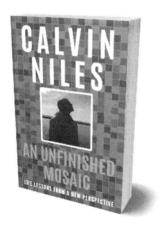

Now available on Amazon

Discover more about Calvin Niles' work

Visit
www.calvinniles.com

Printed in Great Britain
by Amazon